Praise for M

"Wonderful uplifting stor young athlete going through the rigors of growing up with athletic talent, and having parents and others who are involved in his efforts to succeed. Magnificent story about individual personal achievement actually achieved. Very pertinent story for any individual who wants to work to succeed."
Bob Hines, San Diego, CA

For anyone interested in baseball, this could end up being the best series for pure enjoyment to come along in a long time. Following the life of Billy Tankersly has been fun. I enjoyed the first book in the Metal Spikes series, but this is a great second book. I may never get tired of reading this author's work. **Tim Clark, Kansas City, Mo.**

It's a "Field of Dreams." That's what this book is. It's a place where a young boy's mind wanders when he loves baseball as much as Billy Tankersly does. It's a place where we all would like to go, if we had half a chance to. It's a place where Warren Haskin actually takes us in Metal Spikes II. You know what I like best about the book? The author, himself, has walked in those shoes ..... in those spikes that is. How else could he be so, incredibly, detailed about a young player stealing his way through the minor league and sliding into the majors unless he has had that experience himself? And now, I finally got my chance to go there too. I walked that Field of Dreams with the author in reading Metal Spikes I & II.
Jim Losher

Billy Tankersly is back! We've all been waiting to see what it would be like to live as a big leaguer and Warren doesn't disappoint. This book focuses more on the daily life of a kid-turned-baseball star and the way a positive outlook and high-expectations can change your world and the people around you. Billy continues to look to his mentors for inspiration and shows what can happen when you open yourself to the possibilities of a Great Attitude. Warren knocks another one out of the park. Can't wait for the next book in the series. **Bill Hagara**

I don't remember a fictional baseball story about a young man, growing up to play professional baseball before. I'm sure there has been one that I just don't remember, but Metal Spikes I & II are fascinating books, by what I suspect is an up and coming author. **Fred Troutman, Houston, Tx.**

"Another great (and more streamlined) read from Mr. Haskin - full of life lessons. I love all the play-by-plays and feel as if I'm sitting in the stands for each game. All parents need to hand this book to their youngsters, whatever their aspirations."
Catherine Athearn

Billy Tankersly

in

Metal
Spikes
II

Warren Haskin

Billy Tankersly

in

Metal Spikes II

Warren Haskin

Published By
Positive Imaging, LLC
bill@positive-imaging.com

Copyright   2018   Warren Haskin
ISBN   9781944071646

Contents

DEDICATION

I want to dedicate Metal Spikes II to all the Moms and Dads who haul their kids from one game to another. When publishing the first book of the series, I posted a note in "Baseball Moms" on Facebook thanking them, in remembrance of my parents. Two hundred and seventy Moms liked my comment. Their comments inspired me as I wrote Metal Spikes ll and thought about what parents sacrifice; investing time, energy and money into our kids, making our world a better, healthier and more productive place for all.

1

Billy Arrives at Lexington Legends Park

Arriving at the Class A Lexington Legends ballpark, his metal spikes hanging from his shoulders, Billy was ready to start his professional career. Realizing he had achieved his first goal of being a number one draft pick, he now had new goals and felt pressured for one of the few times in his life. As he walked into the Lexington Legends locker room, his uneasiness was not normal. Questions were rolling through his mind. Was he going to be good enough to even reach the majors, let alone break Ricky Henderson's stolen base record? Was he even ready to play professional baseball at only 16 years old?

The Legends were halfway through their season, so the pressure was on Billy to adjust quickly to get into the starting lineup.

"Hey Rookie," one of the players yelled as Billy walked into the clubhouse. Billy was not sure if he was being razzed or if the player was friendly. He found out real fast.

"Come over here and shine my spikes," the young player directed Billy.

"Hi, I'm Billy Tankersly," Billy said as he held his hand out for a handshake.

"I don't think you heard me, rookie.....I need my spikes shined", commanded this apparent bully. Billy wondered if this kid, not much older than him, knew he was talking to a first round pick. Then he thought back to a conversation with his Dad about not getting too cocky and thinking too much of himself.

"What's your name?" Billy asked, ignoring the shoeshine remark.

"Leve Peterson," he answered.

"What position do you play?" Billy asked.

"Left Field, Billy," he responded, holding his knuckles out to Billy.

They bumped fists, and Leve told Billy he was just kidding about the shoeshine remark, but rookies had to have some sort of experience to start their professional baseball career. Billy laughed, sort of a nervous laugh.

Billy was surprised the Royals had started him here in Lexington instead of the Rookie League, where most newly drafted players started.

Leve signed last year, and this was a promotion for him because he started in the Rookie League. As the other players showed up, Leve introduced each of them to Billy, and before he knew it, he was dressed in his Legend's uniform and on the field ready to take batting practice.

It was three hours before game time, and Billy was amazed to see how much preparation went into each game. When it was his turn to take batting practice, the Manager, Coach Vern Wanamaker, came over to talk to Billy.

"Billy, we are really glad to have you here," he started. Pedro Reddington, our shortstop, was injured last week, and we've been short-handed ever since. You think you could start today's game?" the coach quizzed Billy.

The 16-year old did not even blink as he answered, "Absolutely." His outward confidence level was at an all-time high, ever since his name was announced as the Royals first round pick in the draft, but inside, nerves were giving him an upset stomach. This nervousness was a strange feeling for Billy. He stepped into the batting cage and immediately let three pitches go by without swinging. He was waiting for his pitch, wanting to impress the manager. "Billy, do you know what contact hitting is?" the manager said as Billy stepped back away from the plate before the next pitch.

"That's the way the Royals play," answered Billy.

"Yes it is, and it's the way we train here at the Legends," drawled Coach Wanamaker, who apparently was from somewhere in the south. "I want you to hit the next pitch, wherever it is pitched," instructed Billy's first professional coach.

The next pitch was outside, but Billy hit a line drive to left field that rolled into the gap.

"That's what I'm talking about, Billy," the coach yelled, praising Billy.

"The Royals complete minor league system has to learn to hit this way, Billy, because when we make contact, even if we don't hit it hard, it gives us more of a chance to get on base and score runs," Coach Wanamaker explained. "Many major league teams have adopted our way of playing after the Royals won the World Series last year."

"I've always been taught to wait for my pitch," Billy explained to the Coach.

"Yes, Billy, but you are now a professional, and you are going to have to learn to do things differently than you did as an amateur," Coach Wanamaker said.

Billy remembered Mr. Booker, his old mentor, telling him that he had to respect authority, and really listen and learn as coaches tried to teach him. He realized, "This is what Mr. Booker meant," as he hit one ball after another from the cage. No matter where the pitch was unless it was so far from him that he could not make contact, he was swinging and having fun doing it.

2

Billy is Fast and Smart

The game started with nearly 2000 fans in the stands. Billy was starting but hitting eighth in the lineup, something he had never done before. The Legends trailed, 2-0, in the third inning when Billy finally got up to bat. As he had trained himself to do, he had been watching the West Virginia pitcher like a hawk. The West Virginia Power led the South Atlantic League's Northern Division with a 20-10 record while the Legends, Billy's team in the South Division, were crawling along with an 11-19 record.

The pitcher for the Power was Oscar Bratwich, who Billy was going to face in his first professional at-bat. He will never forget Oscar's name and wondered if he would see him in the majors one day. Before stepping into the batter's box, Billy stopped, looked around the field and over to the dugout. This was a memory he wanted to keep forever.

Bratwich started Billy with a curve that broke inside, and Billy let it go for "ball one." He wondered if Coach Wanamaker would have had him swing at that pitch.

The next pitch was a fastball, right over the heart of the plate. Billy saw the ball hit his bat before it darted in the gap between center field and right field. Billy started for second but put the brakes on as the right fielder gobbled it up and had it back to second faster than any outfielder he had ever seen.

"My first professional hit," thought Billy, his heart pounding as he looked to see the signs from the third base coach, Coach Neil, hoping the coaches knew he could steal. The Legends players in the dugout were all cheering for Billy because rookie or not; they wanted to win.

Billy saw the steal sign as Mack Monroe; the second baseman stepped into the box. Mack was a second year player on the Legends, like Leve, and knew to take the first pitch, giving Billy the chance to steal.

He had been watching Bratwich on every pitch, but the only two hits for the Legends, other than Billy's hit, were doubles, so Billy did not have time to study the pitcher's pickoff move.

He took a decent size lead, but one where he knew he could get back safely if Bratwich tried to pick him off. Sure enough, over to first base came a pickoff throw. Billy didn't even bother to dive back. He knew it was Bratwich's warning pickoff, not a real pickoff....and there was a difference as he had learned last year with the Yankees.

Billy took a bigger lead, and before he knew it, Bratwich was throwing to first again. Billy dove, stretching his arm, hand, and fingers to tag the bag before he was tagged out.

"Safe," yelled the ump.

Billy had never seen a pickoff move that fast...and sneaky. He did not hesitate, though, once he saw Bratwich's leg cross the mound on his first pitch to Mack. He was headed to second.

As Billy slid in headfirst, he saw the umpire wave his arms, indicating Billy was safe, but for some reason, he didn't hear him.

Billy had his first professional stolen base. He had already looked up the single-season stolen base record for the Legends and was shocked to find that it belonged to Delino Hopkins, who was in Triple-A this year. Billy had read about Hopkins in the Kansas City Star newspaper where he had been touted as a future Royal.

"OK, only 82 more bases to steal this year," thought Billy, completely forgetting that only 40 games were remaining for the Legends.

On the next pitch, Mack hit a slow dribbler to third base. The third baseman did not even bother to look at Billy assuming he would stay at second base. By the time he picked it up and threw casually to first, Billy was rounding third, on his way to the plate.

The first baseman caught the ball as a routine catch, looking back to second to make sure Billy was still there. By the time he realized Billy was on his way to the plate, his throw was hurried and on the first base side, allowing Billy to slide in safely.

As the ump yelled, "Safe," Billy's new teammates were out of the dugout and giving Billy chest bumps.

That was the spark the Legends needed, and they came back to win 5-3. Billy ended his first professional game with one hit, a walk, and one stolen base. He scored both times he was on base.

It seemed strange to Billy to play a full nine-inning game, but the feeling after a win was good, no matter how many innings they played. With all the excitement in the clubhouse, there was no one more excited than Billy Tankersly. He was a professional ballplayer with a stolen base in his first game.

As he sat by his locker, while changing clothes, he could hardly wait to get back to his temporary living quarters, a hotel on Lexington Street. He hoped they had Wi-Fi so he could Skype his best friend,

Bobby Banks in Austin, Texas, to tell him about his first professional game.

"Hey Bobby, guess what?" Billy started, as soon as he got to his room.

"I don't have to guess, Billy," he declared. "I found the Lexington radio station and listened. Congratulations, Mr. Stolen Base King!"

3

More Enthusiasm

Coach Wanamaker started Billy the next day. They were playing West Virginia Power in the second of a three game series. No one really expected the Legends to win a series the rest of the year, but no one told Billy that. He was as excited about this game as he was the first game. The rest of the team seemed to notice Billy's confidence. They started talking about winning the game, and consequently the series since they were getting more confident after winning the first game.

Billy was still hitting eighth in the lineup. By the time he got up to bat, the Legends led, 1-0 on Tom Jersey's home run (HR) in the second inning. Billy swung on the first pitch and hit a weak grounder to the second baseman. He showed off his speed even if it was for naught. The first base umpire called him "out," and then the next two batters struck out. Going into the top of the fourth inning, the Legends took the field, hustling more than the day before, Billy noticed.

Forest Paige was pitching for the Legends. He shut out West Virginia the first three innings, but Sam Houston, the leadoff batter for the Power, walked on Paige's four pitches. Billy ran in to remind Forest he was the same person who had not allowed a run in the first three innings. Forest smiled, thanked Billy for the encouragement and proceeded to strike out Bill Houston on a 3 & 2 pitch. The next batter hit a sharp grounder to Billy's right that he backhanded before twisting in the air and throwing a bullet to Hank Green, the first baseman. Unfortunately, the throw was low, and Hank could not scoop it up. The runner was safe.

Billy was losing a little of that swagger he brought to the ballpark yesterday. He wondered if he would have been better off throwing to second base for a force out. The official scorer ruled the last play a hit, but Billy knew he should have made a better throw to first or tried to get the force out. Now, with a runner on first and second, West Virginia had their first hope. Their dugout came alive as the number three hitter for the Power was coming up. Tanner Evans, for the Power, had hit 24 HRs this year and was leading the league.

Tanner swung at the first pitch and hit a scorcher to Mack. He picked it up on one bounce and threw to Billy covering second. Billy took the chest-high throw and rifled it to Hank for an inning-ending double play. Once Billy reached the dugout, the team was cheering for him, and it was like the day before. Everyone was excited and ready to win the second game.

Neither team scored in the fifth inning and going into the bottom of the sixth inning, Billy was third up. Leve, who was playing in left field (LF), led off the sixth inning with a single to right field. Brock Snow, the centerfielder, tried to lay a bunt down but popped it up to the pitcher. Leve was still on first base as Billy stepped into the batter's box. After swinging at two pitches that were probably out of the strike zone, Billy was frustrated but determined to get a hit to move Leve over to third base at least.

On the next pitch, Billy swung and missed for strike three. He wanted to throw his bat down, or his hat or something. Instead, he walked back to the dugout where the rest of the team was now cheering for Josh Hampton, the catcher in today's game. Josh hit a blooper to right field that fell in for a hit with Leve going to third base. The Legends dugout was as loud as it had been since Billy joined the team.

With runners on the "corners" first and third bases, Bill Tompkins, the right fielder, and leadoff hitter swung and missed on the first pitch. The dugout was alive now, hoping Bill would get at least a single to drive in Leve, who was doing his best to distract the Powers starting pitcher by pretending to steal home. Bill swung at the next pitch and everyone at the game knew it was a HR. The only one who did not know it was the right fielder for the Power who made a leaping catch at the base of the right field fence. Another inning and no runs for the Legends. Coach Wanamaker decided to let Forrest start the seventh inning, but had Pedro Martinez warming up in the bullpen, in case Forrest got in trouble.

Tanner, the league leading HR hitter for the Power, was first up to bat. Billy wondered if the Coach should have brought in Pedro, but ran to his shortstop (SS) position and took a couple of grounders thrown by Hank, at 1B. Paige's first pitch to Tanner was a fastball over the heart of the plate, and the ball ended up in the parking lot over right field (RF) fence. One pitch by Forrest and the score was tied.

Coach jogged to the mound waving his left hand in the air, meaning Pedro was coming in to relieve Forrest. Billy hadn't seen Pedro pitch, but he had heard about him. He had a fastball that approached 93 mph, and a changeup that hit 73 mph.

Three Power batters later, and Billy saw why Pedro was so effective. Ten pitches and three outs.

On the way to the dugout, Billy ran a little faster to slap Pedro on the back saying "Way to go, Pedro."

It was the last of the ninth inning before Billy got up again, but this time the Legends had runners on first and third with only one out. Going back to his earlier years, Billy remembered several times where he had the chance to be the hero and win the game, especially the Yankee's game where he tried too hard to hit a homer and struck out.

"Not this time," thought Billy. Coach Neil, the third base coach, gave Billy a signal he did not remember. Billy called timeout and walked over to Coach Neil to tell him he was sorry, but he did not recognize the signal the coach gave him.

"Billy, I was going to have you execute a squeeze bunt, but now they might suspect it since you had to come ask me," the coach whispered. "OK, I want you to swing hard at the first pitch like you are going for a HR, but miss it on purpose." Then on the second pitch, I'm going to have Brock do a delayed steal, which means you have to bunt the ball because Brock will be thrown out if you don't make contact with the ball," explained the coach. "As soon as you bunt it, Brock will be on his way to the plate."

On the first pitch, Billy swung for the fences but missed the ball by a foot, as it had been a changeup and dropped far below Billy's bat. Billy stepped back into the box. He turned around, looked at the catcher, and muttered, "I'll be ready for his changeup the next time he throws it."

The next pitch was another changeup, over the heart of the plate, perfect for a bunt. Billy squared around and dropped a bunt down the third base line. Brock scored easily to give the Legends their second win in two days. The team ran to the center of the infield and started giving each other high fives as they headed back to the dugout. They had just beaten the league leaders' two straight games and still had another game tomorrow night. Both games so far had been day games, but tomorrow night would be Billy's first professional game under the lights.

4

Billy's First Bus Ride in the Minor Leagues

Game three of the series with the West Virginia Power did not turn out as well as Billy had hoped. He struck out twice and hit a grounder to the second basemen in his only other trip to the plate. The Legends lost 6-3. What happened next surprised Billy? The team was told to get packed as the Legends' team bus would be leaving in one hour. Billy had read about how the minor leaguers traveled by bus, but it had not dawned on him that the team would be catching the bus right after the game was over.

Billy got his equipment, ran to his hotel on Lexington Street, and just barely made it back to the bus. It resembled an old school bus, and Billy wondered if it would get out of the parking lot.

But sure enough it sputtered along and once it was in third gear seemed to ride fine. Billy sat next to Mack Monroe, who had become his best friend in the first three days. They talked about how they could make their double plays better. Mack told Billy that he liked to receive the throws on a double play to his right so he could transfer the ball out in one motion. After about 30 minutes of talking with Mack, Billy realized he didn't even know where they were going. So he asked Mack sheepishly.

"You've got to be kidding, Billy," laughed Mack. "We are headed to Greenville, North Carolina to play the Greenville Drive. They are in third place in our division, the South Atlantic League Southern." Billy asked how many games they would be playing at Greenville.

"We've got a four game series with them, and then we go to Asheville, North Carolina, just a short hop skip and jump from Greenville. Asheville is below us in the standings now as they lost their last three games," Mack explained to Billy, who was all ears.

They arrived at the hotel a little after 3:00 AM. Coach Wanamaker told the team to be at the park by 2:00 PM as it was a 6:05 PM start to the game.

Billy could not go to sleep. He was still thinking about his bunt that won the second game. Naturally, everyone had complimented him on a perfect squeeze bunt, but he realized he had not gotten a chance to steal a base in the second or third game. He fell asleep thinking he was going to steal 2B and 3B in the first game against the Greenville Drive.

The series in Greenville seemed to be over before it started. Billy had one hit and one stolen base in the first game but went hitless in the remaining three games. The Legends won two out of the four games and was on the bus for a short trip to Asheville, where they would play the Tourists in a three game series.

It seemed they had just arrived in Greenville, but then, back on the bus again, headed to another city he had never been to. The bus ride was not as smooth as it was coming to Greenville. He didn't know if it was the road or the bus that was so rough, but he felt for the older players because his back was sore from the ride. It wasn't his back pain that occupied his brain. All Billy could think about was going 0 for 11 in the last three games in Greenville. He had been making contact with the ball, but each time the ball shot directly into the glove of the opposing team for an out. He was surprised to see the "shift" put on, even in the minors. He knew the coaches had data of all kinds, and by now, they had a good idea where Billy was going to hit it. Still, 0 for 11 was not something Billy had ever encountered before. Sitting beside Mack on the bus, Billy told him that going 0-11 was something that had never happened to him before.

"Billy, you might as well get used to it because when you play as many games as we do, it is going to happen. Don't be surprised if you get six or seven hits in the Asheville series," Mack encouraged the young Billy Tankersly. He also told Billy something extremely important. He had to learn to hit the ball where they were not. If they shifted to the right side of the diamond, he had to learn to hit to the left side. He was surprised that this was the first time he had been taught that in all his years in baseball. But, he'd never faced a shift in traveling baseball, so Billy figured this was just part of the difference between amateur ball and the pro's.

5

How To End A Slump

Billy was surprised at how beautiful the Asheville stadium was. He studied the field before their first game; an hour before anyone else from either team showed up. Billy was thirsty for success. He was taught to visualize what he wanted. As he sat in the dugout, he pictured getting his first HR in professional baseball in this stadium. It was only 320 feet to the right field fence. He visualized hitting a fastball, far over the fence to get everyone's attention.

When Coach Wanamaker arrived and saw Billy suited up in the dugout. He walked over, smiled and sat down next to Billy.

"Billy, I know you were 0-11 your last three games in Greenville. Sometimes, that can destroy the confidence of a young player. However, let me give you some advice. You must put that behind you and only look ahead," taught the manager. "In fact, in baseball, you can never look back because there are too many 0-11's over the course of a season. I know you've learned how to control your emotions by now, but are you looking forward?" asked Coach Wanamaker.

"Yes, Coach," responded Billy. I fully understand the importance of visualizing what you want. I learned a long time ago, from my Dad in fact, that a baseball player fails far more than he succeeds. That is what I have been doing the last hour, visualizing the results of today's game and the entire series. Watch me get my first HR, Coach," smiled Billy, "and watch us win the series."

When the rest of the team had arrived, gone through hitting and fielding practice, the manager announced the lineup. Billy was hitting seventh which he found to be a little odd after going 0-11. It showed that Coach Wanamaker had faith in what he had seen from Billy.

By the time Billy came up to bat in the third inning, Asheville lead, 2-0. He was leading off. Even though Billy had been visualizing hitting a HR, he realized that the Legends needed baserunners more than a single HR.

"Ball one," called the umpire in a voice that sounded more like a whisper. After taking two more pitches, both balls, Billy stood at the plate with a 3-0 count. He looked to the third base coach to see if he had the "take" sign on, meaning he would not swing in hopes the pitcher would throw another ball. Sure enough, he saw the coach wipe his hands across his chest and then touch both arms. Billy knew that was the "take" sign.

The Asheville pitcher had not walked anyone yet and was visibly upset with the last call by the umpire. Billy knew the next pitch would be a fastball, over the heart of the plate. He stepped in the box, and just as the pitcher was about ready to get the sign from the catcher, Billy stepped out of the box. He was trying to upset the pitcher even more. It worked. The ball was so far out of the strike zone that Billy was almost laughing as he ran down to first. He was pretty sure Coach Neil would not give him the steal sign since the Legends needed two runs.

Brock Snow was at the plate as Billy looked at the third base coach just in case he gave him the steal sign. Instead, he gave the "take" sign to Brock. Asheville had heard about Billy's first game of scoring on an infield out, so they knew he was fast. The pitcher threw a "pitch out," hoping Billy would try to steal. Brock let it go by for "ball one," and Billy did not go. On the next pitch, Billy saw the steal sign from his coach. His heart beat faster. Taking an eight-foot lead was enough to get the Asheville pitcher's attention. Billy dove back to the bag as the pick-off attempt was almost a wild pitch into right field, but the 1B scooped it up, keeping Billy on first. The catcher called a timeout, walked to the mound, said something to the pitcher, and ran back behind the plate.

The next pitch was a fastball over the plate, and Billy took off for second base. The catcher made a motion to second base but didn't even throw the ball as Billy slid in head first not realizing there was not going to be a throw. Among the things he learned from Coach Booker was never to look back on a steal attempt. He now had his second stolen base of his professional career, and Billy was as excited about this one as he had been after his first steal.

Brock now had a 1-1 count and drove the next pitch to deep left field. The left fielder caught the ball near the fence, and Billy started racing to third, but with the fielder in his line of sight, he knew better than to test the arm of a fielder he'd never seen before. The ball came quickly into third base and would have beaten Billy. Coach Neil realized at that point, Billy was more mature than most of the players on the team. He smiled at Billy, giving him a thumbs-up for not trying to reach third base.

Josh Hamilton, the catcher, was batting ninth and laced a single to right field. Billy saw the coach swinging his arms wildly, telling Billy to keep running. He did not hesitate as he rounded third base.

He scored easily as the throw to the plate was over the catcher's head, and Josh ended up on second base. The rest of the team was showing more enthusiasm than during the first couple of innings now that they had scored.

Mack singled in Josh, and the rout was on. Five more batters came to the plate before Ashville had recorded an out. The Legends scored five runs and never trailed the rest of the game.

After the win, eating a burger back at the hotel, Mack and Billy excitedly discussed the game. Billy grounded out his second time at the plate and then his third time up, he hit one over the 320-foot sign in right field for his first professional HR! He did not get any other hits, but Mack could not stop talking about Billy's long HR.

"Billy, I heard you talking to the coach before the game about visualizing. I've heard about it; does it work for you" Mack asked.

"Well, I learned a long time ago that to achieve anything, you have to believe that you've already received it," started Billy. "I sat in the dugout before the game, visualizing hitting one over that short fence."

"Do you mean you just imagined it?" asked Mack.

"Well, sort of," answered Billy. "I actually believed I was going to hit it out of the park. I pictured it in my mind. I even said out loud that I was going to hit a homer, this game."

"Billy, you were something like 0-10 or 0-11 before this game," started Mack, with what Billy knew was going to be another question about him actually believing he was going to hit a homer.

"How were you able to believe?" quizzed Mack "I just don't understand."

"Mack, if we want anything in life, we have to believe we are going to get it before we actually receive it," stated Billy. "It's like, you don't think about what happens when you turn a light switch on, but you know the light will come on. That's because of repetition. We've turned that switch on so many times, we just expect it to come on. I sat in the dugout an hour before anyone else arrived today. The entire time, I pictured in my mind that I was going to break my slump with a line drive over that short fence," continued the rookie, who was giving advice to a player older and more experienced than him. Billy wondered how anyone could reach this level and not understand visualizing.

"Billy, did you actually see it?" Mack asked, not fully understanding.

"Yes Mack, in my mind, I knew I was going to hit a HR today," answered Billy.

The conversation ended with both young players determined to win the last game in Asheville.

6

Coming Back Home To Lexington

The last game ended with Billy getting three hits while stealing two bases, and the Legends were going home with the best record they'd had all year, 15-21, only six games under .500.

The bus ride was long, and Billy sat next to Leve, the first player he met as he walked into the clubhouse two weeks ago.

"Billy, you've really added a spark to the team," Leve said, praising Billy. "We've only lost one game since you arrived. Maybe you are our good luck charm," smiled Leve.

"Yeah, we've got a good team," Billy responded. "I'll bet that we have at least three on the team who will one day be on the Royals," he added.

"Who do you think will make it," asked Leve, hoping to hear his name as one of the three.

"You and Mack both have a good shot at reaching the bigs," said Billy, realizing that in all his conversations, he'd never said "the bigs," meaning the major league.

"Since you said, three on the team, and you've only named two, I guess you included yourself," Leve chided.

"Absolutely, I have a goal to make it by the time I'm 20 years old, at the latest. I'm hoping to be playing in Kauffman Stadium in three years," said Billy, matter of factly.

As the bus rolled into Lexington, Coach Wanamaker came to Billy, telling him that he would be rooming with Leve at the Williams residence.

"You mean we live in someone's house?" asked Billy.

"Yes Billy, at this level we cannot afford to put everyone up in a hotel, so people in Lexington offer a bedroom or two in their homes for you guys," explained the Coach.

"The Williams are avid fans, never miss a game, and as part of their contributions back to Lexington, they offer every year to house one or two of the players," the coach continued.

The team got off the bus, and a car was waiting for Leve and him. It was the Williams and their daughter. No one told him about their 17 year old daughter. Billy had not had a girlfriend since Abby. That was when he decided that a girlfriend would just distract him from what he really wanted....to break Ricky Henderson's stolen base record. But Emma Williams got his attention with a smile that would make anyone melt. He melted, even if she was a year older than Billy.

They all went inside, and Mrs. Williams took them to their room. It was upstairs and had a big window with the ballpark in the distance.

"Hey Leve, you never mentioned about Emma," Billy teased.

"Billy, I figured you'd just fall in love and forget all about baseball," kidded Leve.

"Baseball?" Billy joked. "What's that?"

Leve laughed and told Billy he was going to hit the sack. Both boys laid down, but Billy couldn't go to sleep. He got up, went out to the front porch to call Bobby, his best friend ever, who was still playing on a traveling team out of Houston.

"Hey Bobby," Billy laughed.

"I knew you were on the road and were in a 0-11 slump, so I didn't want to call you," Bobby answered.

"It's a lot different here, Bobby," Billy explained. "I'd heard about how tough low minor league ball was, but holy smokes, we have not had a day off since I joined the team."

"We play again tomorrow night, which means I can sleep in tomorrow morning, and that will be very welcomed," stated Billy. "But we still have to be at the ballpark by 2:00 PM for our night game."

"How are you playing, Bobby?" Billy asked.

"Well, I'm leading the league in HR's and have had three scouts talk to me," answered Bobby.

"You will be in the minors next year, so just count on it," Billy encouraged.

"Yeah, but I won't be a number one draft pick like you," laughed Bobby.

"Hey, don't talk like that, Bobby. I'd bet you $5.00 that you will be signed in the first two rounds," encouraged Billy even more.

"Bobby, I've got to tell you, we don't live in hotels at this level, but in people's homes. I'm living with the Williams family in Lexington, and they have a girl by the name of Emma. She's really nice, Bobby; I think I'm in love," smiled Billy as he told his friend about Emma. "OK, I've got to get to bed to be ready for tomorrow but wanted to talk to you before I hit the sack," Billy ended the conversation.

7

An Unexpected Surprise

The Legends were going to be playing the Columbia Fireflys, who were in last place in the Southern Division. Mr. Williams drove Leve and Billy to the ballpark and Billy was surprised beyond belief. Standing outside the clubhouse was his Dad, Mom, and Mr. Booker.

He went running to them, hugging them all like he'd never seen them before.

"Son, we would have been here sooner, but after talking it over with your Mom and Mr. Booker, we all decided that it was best to let you get your feet wet before we came to a game," Billy's Dad said.

"We did expect a call or something," his Mom broke in.

"Mom, I don't think I was mentally prepared for the past two weeks. This is hard, riding a semi-school bus halfway across the country," Billy actually teared up as he hugged his Mom with a bear hug that made her realize he was still her little boy.

After another round of hugs from his Dad and Mr. Booker, Billy told them he had to go suit up for practice and the game that night.

He left them outside of the clubhouse, realizing he'd missed them more than he imagined. He'd been so focused on playing well that every time he thought to call them, something else happened to bring his thoughts back to the game that day or the game the next day.

Inside the clubhouse, Leve asked him if that was his Dad and Mother.

"It was, Leve, plus Mr. Booker, who I think I told you about," answered Billy.

"Is he the guy who taught you about visualizing?" Leve asked.

"Yep, the best coach ever," responded Billy with a smile, knowing it was his Dad who taught him about visualizing. But, it did remind him all that Mr. Booker had meant to him. During batting practice, Billy was hitting the ball all over the park. He felt good.

Billy was excited to have his Dad, Mom, and Mr. Booker see how well he and Mack turned double plays. In two short weeks, these two had developed into what an opposing coach said was the best double play combo in the league. They knew they were getting better with each passing game.

The game wasn't even close. Billy had two hits and two stolen bases, which made him proud that he had two steals in a game with his family and Mr. Booker watching. The final score was 8-2, and the Legends were now only five games below .500 with a 16-21 record. What Billy had not realized was the season was divided into two halves, and the Legends had a chance to win the second half of the Southern Division.

"Guys, we really need to sweep the Fireflys." Coach Wanamaker started telling the team about the importance and urgency of this game. "If we win these remaining two games, we will have a real good shot at winning the second half and get into the playoffs," the coach told the team.

Billy knew that they not only needed to win these final two games against the Fireflys but get a streak of five or six wins to ensure they could make the playoffs. They would be playing the Rome Braves in

Lexington before going on the road. Billy enjoyed coming back to the Williams home after games and talking to Emma. She seemed to be almost as interested in baseball and stats as Billy. The Braves were three games above .500, so the Legends needed to sweep them as well as the Fireflys.

Billy found himself hitting sixth when Coach Wanamaker announced the starting lineup. The first inning was uneventful with neither team scoring or getting a hit. Billy was third up in the second inning, and he hoped Leve or Bill Ostoff could get on base in front of him so he could drive them in.

Leve hit a line drive that the SS on the Fireflys leaped high and timed it perfectly to make a great play for the out. Billy O, the nickname for Bill Ostoff was up next and hit a ball into the gap between right and center field, and slid into second base before the ball arrived. Billy had a chance to drive in the game's first run.

He took his time before stepping into the box, the same way he had before his first game, studying the surroundings in the ballpark. He was really looking for his parents and Mr. Booker this time though. He spotted them about four rows back of the Legends dugout. He realized this was only the second professional game his folks and Mr. Booker had seen him play, and when he did finally step into the batter's box, he was determined to get a hit to score Billy O.

"Strike One," bellowed the ump on the first pitch that Billy thought was outside. He dug his metal spikes into his comfortable position and glared at the pitcher. It was almost impossible for a 16 year old kid to intimidate a guy who had been playing at this level for two years, but the look in Billy's eyes was definitely noticeable to the Firefly's pitcher.

The next pitch was way outside, so the count was now 1-1. He expected a curve and was completely fooled by a fastball that caught the corner of the plate. "Strike Two," yelled the ump.

Billy was determined to at least hit the ball. He was not going to strike out. He fouled off the next two pitches. The count was still 1-2. He was determined. Jumping back on the next pitch, he avoided being hit with an inside fastball. He knew it was an intended pitch, and the next pitch would probably be a curve.

Billy remembered to watch the spin on the ball. "Ball Three," barked the ump. 3 and 2 count and Billy expected a fastball.

He got all of it. The sound of the ball hitting the bat was a sound that avid baseball fans knew. There was no doubt. As Billy ran toward first, he watched the ball clear the right field fence for a home run. As he rounded third base, he looked into the stands after hearing a familiar voice. It was good to hear his Mom's voice. Billy O- was waiting at the plate with a high-five. The team was not far behind.

During the rest of the game, the Legends continued hitting. With a 7-1 lead, Billy got up again. He singled with a line drive over the 2B. Because of the big lead, he was pretty sure he would not get the steal sign, and his instincts were correct. The game ended with that same score.

Billy was proud that he'd played a good game on offense and defense in front of his folks. He and Mack turned two double plays, with him starting one and Mack starting the other. They gave each other high fives after the last one as it ended the game.

Billy got dressed and met his folks and Mr. Booker outside of the ballpark.

"You want to grab a bite to eat?" his dad asked.

"Sure," Billy replied. Can Mack come with us?"

His folks and Mr. Booker sounded really happy that Billy had met someone he wanted to take to dinner with the family that night. They thought back to his decisions along the way to leave one team and join the traveling baseball team. They knew how much he missed his friends when he first joined the traveling team. They hoped Mack was as good a player as Billy and would work his way up the ranks along with their son.

There was a Luby's Buffet in Lexington, and when his folks suggested they go there, Billy was excited because he'd spent the last two weeks, eating food that was good for him. He knew he did not have the willpower to pass up the chicken fried steak and cream gravy at Luby's.

"Hey Mack, tell my folks about the Greyhound bus we take from city to city," laughed Billy over dinner.

Mack cracked up and started bouncing up and down in his chair. Everyone in the restaurant probably thought he was nuts, although Billy's folks understood.

They all had a good time, but Billy had one more thing he wanted to do with his folks that night. He wanted to introduce them to the Williams and Emma, so after dinner, they drove to the Williams home.

Emma was out on a date. Billy was disappointed that she didn't get to meet his parents, but the Williams told Billy's folks what a fine young man they raised. He was proud, but maybe not as much as his folks. Before leaving, they thanked the Williams for all they did for Billy and the rest of the team by being loyal supporters and making their home available to the young players each year.

Billy said goodbye to his folks. He was excited they were there, but his mind was already on the next day's game. He knew the Fireflys were throwing a lefty against the Legends, and Billy had gone 0-6 against lefties since joining the team. As he drifted off to sleep that night, he was visualizing hitting two singles off the lefty.

Coach Wanamaker held a meeting in the clubhouse before the game.

"Fellows, we've got a good streak going, but we need to win the next four to really have a chance, and it starts today, one game at a time."

By the time the game ended, the Legends had destroyed the lefty starting pitcher as he gave up five runs in the first two innings. Billy ended his "O fer" streak with three singles and three stolen bases. He stole second and third in the fifth inning and was gaining the respect of the opposing pitchers as they tried to hold him closer to the bag, than any team so far. It made no difference. Billy was so fast that he felt he could steal a base every time he came to the plate.

Billy forgot to tell his folks that they had to board the bus right after the game. They had a chance to give him a hug and encouragement before the bus took off for Hickory, North Carolina to play the Hickory Crawdads, who were in second place in the Northern Division. It was going to be tough to win three against them.

8

The Team's Streak Continues

The Legends beat the Crawdads three straight by scores of 4-2, 3-2 and 6-5; all close games that could have gone either way. But for the moment, the Legends were on a winning streak that had them moving up in the standings to second in their division. They were now at .500, 21-21. Billy had four hits in the series, and Mack had three with one being a HR. The two boys had become good friends sharing stories of home and family and people who had helped them along the way. Billy felt like he had a whole new family.

The next three games were against the Greensboro Grasshoppers, which was only 98 miles from Hickory. Greensboro won the South Atlantic League last year and was in first place again this year. It was going to be hard to beat them three straight, but Coach Wanamaker told the team before the first game that they were playing the best baseball in the league. He then motivated them with a story.

"Guys, Coach Tammic of the Crawdads told me that every team in the league did not want to play the Legends right now," Coach Wanamaker started.

"Everyone in the league is fearful of you guys," the coach continued. "I don't think you realize yet just how good you are. There is no doubt in my mind that you can sweep the Grasshopers three straight," the coach concluded.

The first game went extra innings. Billy came up in the top of the tenth inning and hit a blooper over the second baseman's head that fell in for a single.

He knew he was going to get a steal sign, and he was correct in his thinking because, on the first pitch, he got it!

"You are never going to be able to steal on Henry," the first baseman said to Billy before the pitch. Billy just looked at him, like "watch me." He got a 10-foot lead, knowing this Henry guy was going to try to pick him off. With a quick throw to first, Billy was back in plenty of time, but he did dive head first to make sure.

Then He got his normal 10-foot lead, and as soon as Henry's foot passed the mound, Billy was off. Digging as hard as he could, he could tell from the second baseman covering the bag, it was going to be close. He dove, reaching the bag with his left hand and slid across the base.

"Safe!" yelled the umpire. Billy got up, dusted himself off and looked to Coach Neil for another steal sign. If he could only reach 3B safely, a sacrifice fly could score him, but there was no steal sign.

Leve was at the plate, and apparently, the coach had faith in him getting a hit, or he would have given Billy the steal sign again. On the first pitch, a slider dropped straight down, Levi jumped out of the way, and the ball was got by the catcher. Billy was off for third base immediately.

Again, he was safe and with no outs; all Levi had to do was hit a fly ball to any of the outfielders and Billy knew he could score. On the next pitch, Levi hit a soft fly ball to center. The centerfielder caught the ball on the run toward the plate to get his throw off as fast as possible.

Billy ran. It was a good throw. Billy dove on the inside of the plate, touching it with his left hand as he slid past the plate. He was sure he'd beaten the throw.

"Yrrr Out," the umpire yelled. Billy got up and started arguing with the umpire, claiming the catcher missed the tag. Coach Neil ran in from the third base coaching box to argue with the umpire, but really to get between Billy and the umpire so Billy would not be tossed out of the game.

Now there were two outs as Hank Green, the first baseman came to bat. On the first pitch, he hit one of the longest balls Billy had seen hit since joining the professional ranks. The ball cleared the center-field fence by at least 20 feet, and the Legends had the lead in the top of the tenth.

In the bottom of the tenth, Sam Houston came into relieve and immediately struck out the side. The Legends' winning streak continued, and they were now one game above .500 at 22-21.

The second and third games were not close at all as the Legends players seem to realize they might be the best team in the league right now, not in the standings but the way they were playing.

9

Playing The First Half Champions

Everyone on the team was contributing, and now they were off on another road trip, this time to Charleston, the most extended trip of the year. Not only was it the longest trip of the year, the Charleston Riverdogs, a minor league team of the New York Yankees, had won the first half of the season. They had a six game lead on the next best team in the second half. Billy had looked up the team on the internet the last night at the Williams. He learned they set a new attendance record for the league last year and were headed to beat that mark this year.

Billy and Mack talked for a little while on the bus trip, and eventually, both dropped off to sleep. They drove all night and didn't reach Charleston until the sun was up. It was a cheap hotel in Charleston, but at least they had Wi-Fi. After sleeping most of the night on the bus, Billy was wide awake as they pulled into Charleston and settled into the hotel, which was initially an apartment complex. Billy walked out to the pool and checked to see if there were any messages from Bobby. He hadn't talked to his best friend in weeks, and even though it was early in the morning, Billy wanted to call Bobby.

"What's up, Billy?" Bobby asked, obviously just getting out of bed.

"We're in Charleston right now, getting ready to play the Riverdogs tonight," Billy told Bobby.

"Wow, you do know who played on the Riverdogs two years ago, don't you?" Bobby asked.

"No," responded Billy.

"Lee Tomelin, the rookie on the Yankees who has hit 40 HRs this year," Bobby explained. "Holy Smokes, if he made it from this league to the majors in two years, I can do the same," Billy laughed.

"Well, I might beat you, Billy," said Bobby in a matter of fact way.

"What. Are you getting signed?" Billy quizzed.

"Not yet, Billy, but I lead the traveling league down here in Texas with 34 home runs and the scouts have been noticing," Bobby said.

"Wouldn't that be great, to be back on the same team as teammates again," Billy thought out loud.

"Count on it, Billy. I'm going to be right behind you," chided Bobby.

The two boys got off the phone, both feeling encouraged in talking to the other. "Best Friends forever," Billy thought.

Billy slept a couple of hours but headed to the ballpark ahead of everyone else. He'd read about Riley Field being voted the nicest field in the league for four straight years. When he arrived, he saw why.

It was by far the most beautiful field Billy had seen as a professional player. The grass infield looked like a green on a golf course, perfectly cut, while the outfield looked like the fairways on a golf course. The grandstands had three levels, and he understood why they were such a good team. Not only were they a Yankees farm club, but they also had fans that really supported the team.

As the game was about to begin, Coach Wanamaker called the team together in the dugout after infield practice.

"OK, this is the one we've been shooting for all year," the coach began. "I know some of you have never played against the Riverdogs, but believe me, they are good," continued the coach. "But we are better," Coach Wanamaker concluded. The game started at 7:05, sharp, with the visiting Legends team batting first.

Bill Tomkins, the right fielder, led off with a single up the middle. Josh Hamilton had been moved up in the lineup and was hitting second. On the first pitch, he sent a ball over the left field fence to give the Legends a 2-0 lead in the first inning. The next three batters struck out. Apparently, the Legends got to the Riverdogs number one pitcher before he was really warmed up.

Sergio Gomez was pitching for the Legends, and it turned out to be the best game he'd ever pitched. Going into the seventh inning, the RiverDogs only had one hit, and the Legends still led 2-0.

Sergio walked the first Riverdog to face him in the bottom of the seventh, and Coach Wanamaker walked to the mound slowly, giving Pedro Gonzales, the relief pitcher, time to throw a couple more pitches in the bullpen. Coach Wanamaker raised his left arm, meaning Pedro was coming in.

Even the Riverdogs fans gave Sergio a nice ovation as he walked off the field. Mack held his glove up over his face and told Billy that he would cover second base on a steal attempt.

Pedro had a big breaking ball, perfect for a grounder, to get a double play. On the first pitch, the RiverDog batter hit a sharp grounder to Billy's right. He backhanded it and was able to throw sidearm to Mack. Mack hit the bag and rifled the ball to first for a double play. Two outs now as their big DH hitter strode to the batter's box.

It only took one pitch to have the Legends lead cut in half. The RiverDogs DH hitter hit one over the centerfield fence, and Brock didn't even turn around. The double play on the pitch before saved the River-Dogs from taking the lead. Pedro struck the next batter out on three pitches. Going to the top of the eighth, the Legends led, 2-1.

Billy was third up in the eighth, and he just hoped to get on base so he could steal. Billy Ostoff found a hole between 3B and SS and was on 1B with no outs. Hank Green stepped into the box ready to drive one out of the park. On the first pitch, he swung so hard he dropped to his knee. Everyone in the park knew he wanted to hit it out of the park, including the RiverDogs pitcher.

Billy was standing in the on-deck circle, swinging a heavy bat, to make his bat at the plate feel light when he got up. Two pitches later, Hank hit a groundball to the SS, making it easy for the River Dogs to turn a double play. Two outs, no one on as Billy walked to the plate.

He remembered the coach telling him "the Legends play contact baseball," and he was ready to hit anything. But four pitches later, he was on 1B with a walk. Looking over to Coach Neil, he got what he wanted the entire game, the steal sign. He took his standard lead off first, figuring the pitcher would try a pickoff before throwing to the plate. Surprisingly, the pitcher stretched looked over at Billy, and quick-pitched Tom Jersey, the DH for the Legends.

"Strike one," yelled the ump. Billy was still standing at 1B. Coach Neil looked at him with a question mark in his eye. Billy had been expecting a pickoff, and the quick pitch kept him from even thinking about running. Now he was ready, and Coach Neil gave him the steal sign again.

He was so fast that the catcher didn't even bother to throw to 2B to get him.

"If Tom can get a hit any place, I'll be able to score," Billy thought to himself. He looked over at Coach Neil and did a double take. He just gave Billy the steal sign again! Billy knew there was no point in reaching 3B with two outs, but there was the sign. He took a slightly bigger lead. When the pitcher's foot crossed the mound, Billy was digging toward third as fast as he could, diving into the base on the outside again, catching the bag with his left hand.

"Safe," called out the umpire. Billy called timeout as he got up and dusted himself off. Coach Neil whispered to him, "Watch for a curve that gets by the catcher." At that point, Billy knew why the coach had him steal third. Because of his speed, if any ball got by the catcher, Billy was to take off running. He looked at the catcher trying to see the sign he was giving to the RiverDogs pitcher, but he wasn't able to see around his knee. Then he looked at the pitcher, trying to see if he was turning the ball in his glove, which might mean the pitch would be a curve. As usual, Billy was studying everything.

The pitcher went into a full windup since Billy was now at third base. The pitch was a fastball. Tom let it go as it was outside. The ump called it a ball. But, because he had now seen two fastballs, Tom expected the next pitch to be a curve. Billy had come to the same conclusion and was ready to run if it got by the catcher at all. The pitch bounced in front of the plate and then bounced off the catcher's glove about ten feet to his right. Billy was off for home when the ball bounced in front of the plate. He knew he was safe. The Legends now had a 3-1 lead with Tom still at the plate. He hit a wicked line drive right at the third baseman for the final out.

The game ended with the Legends getting another win. The team celebrated on the field, giving each other high fives, knowing they could well be on their way to winning the second half as they now were 25-21.

Before heading home to Lexington, the Legends won two more games from the RiverDogs bringing their record to 27-21 and leading the second half standings in their division.

10

A Big Surprise

Back at home in Lexington, the Legends were starting to believe in themselves, even more. Not only that, the grandstands were full by the time the game started. The Augusta GreenJackets were in for a surprise as the Legends won the series and scored sixteen runs while the Legends' pitchers only allowed three runs the entire series. They were now 30-21, a complete change from when Billy joined the team.

It was not going unnoticed by the Kansas City Royals front office, including the General Manager, Dillar Schwartz.

Talking to the KC manager, Skip O'Neil, Dillar started talking about Billy.

"Skip, have you noticed what our first round draft pick has been doing?" the GM asked.

"How could we miss it, Dillar?" Skip said. "The last report I saw had Billy Tankersly hitting .325 with fourteen stolen bases already."

"I think we need to schedule him for the Arizona Fall League," Dillar told the manager.

"Are you sure, Dillar?" Skip questioned out loud. "He's only 16 still, and this is his first year of pro ball."

"To be honest, Skip, I'm not sure, but have a gut level feeling about this kid," Dillar replied.

"I think the experience of the Arizona Fall League will tell us, one way or another if he is ready to be promoted next year," Dillar continued. "I'm going to call Coach Wanamaker tomorrow to see what he thinks," the GM concluded.

Before the first game at home against the Green-Jackets, Coach Wanamaker took the call from the GM of the parent club.

"Hi Coach," Dillar began. "I've been following the youngster who joined your team halfway through the season, this Billy Tankersly kid," the GM continued. "We are toying with the idea of inviting him to play on our Arizona Fall League team once your season is over," said Dillar. "Oh, by the way, great second half the Legends are having," he continued.

"Thanks, Dillar for the compliment on the team this year," Coach Wanamaker replied about the team initially before answering his GM about Billy Tankersly.

"About Billy, the kid is terrific," started Coach Wanamaker. "He is constantly learning, studying the opposing team, the field and is putting the knowledge to good use," the coach starting telling Dillar about Billy.

"He's hitting .333 now, and that is after going 0-11 in a slump at the start of his career," Coach Wanamaker explained. "The kid is ready to be promoted now, Dillar," the coach continued. "He'd been invaluable as a spark plug for the team, in fact, I honestly think the team's record right now reflects more on Billy than my managing to tell you the truth."

"So you think he can hold his own in Arizona?" the GM asked.

"Without a doubt," the coach answered.

"Good Luck the rest of the season," Dillar concluded. He added, "You can tell Billy after tonight's game that we'd like him to join us in the Arizona Fall League."

Billy's game wasn't even close. The home fans were going wild as the Legends scored six runs in the first two innings. Billy had a single and a stolen base, plus scoring a run. The game ended with the Legends winning 10-1, and Billy added two more hits and another stolen base. He was feeling about as good as any 16-year old could feel, not realizing the news he was about to receive.

"Billy, I'd like to see you in my office," the coach announced in the clubhouse after the game.

Billy didn't know whether to be scared or what, but he had never been invited to the coach's office before, so he was a little nervous.

As he walked to Coach Wanamaker's office, he kept replaying the game in his head. Had he missed a signal, had he not hustled to the coach's liking?

"Billy, I've got some good news for you, maybe even great news," the coach started.

"The GM from the Royals called me today, and they would like for you to play in the Arizona Fall League after our season is over," Coach Wanamaker smiled as he was giving Billy the news.

"Are you kidding me, coach?" Billy asked. His mouth dropped open, and he could feel the adrenaline hit his chest.

"Not at all, Billy, the Royals have noticed how you've helped the team while putting up good stats of your own," said the coach, with a tint of enthusiasm in his voice.

Billy was thrilled beyond words. He knew about the Arizona Fall League. He knew that the players invited to play in that short Fall season league were players they felt would make the Royals shortly. He didn't think there was a chance for that, but still, to be invited to play with players who might make the Royals next year was an exciting thought.

Everyone on the team had left, so Billy decided to call his folks with the news and then Mr. Booker. All were excited for him, but no one was going to be as excited as his next call.

"Hey Bobby, how are things in Austin?" Billy started.

After listening to Bobby tell him that he'd been talking to scouts from four different teams now, and how he felt he was going to be drafted in the first or second round, Billy broke the news to Bobby about Arizona.

"Bobby, you won't believe what happened tonight," Billy chirped, like a bird singing a special song. "I've been invited to play in the Arizona Fall League," Billy finally blurted out.

"In the Arizona Fall League?" Bobby repeated in the form of a question. And a comment.

"It was a real surprise to me, Bobby, but the manager called me into his office and told me the Royals wanted to see me there," Billy rattled off in a manner convincing himself that it was true.

"That is so great, Billy," Bobby responded. "You'll do great."

With that, Billy told his friend he had to get to bed but wanted to share the news with his best friend.

11

The League Championship

With Billy leading the way, the Legends won enough games to face the Greensboro Grasshoppers, who had won the first half, in the league championship series. It was a five game series, starting in Greensboro for the first two games, and then to Lexington for three games. The first game went to the Grasshoppers, 5-4. Billy singled twice, stole second twice, and scored two runs, but the Grasshoppers relief pitcher shut the Legends down in the ninth inning to preserve a one run win.

The second game started with the Legends scoring two runs in the first inning. The 2-0 lead held up until the seventh inning when Greensboro scored three runs on two doubles and a HR by the Grasshoppers SS.

Going into the top of the eighth, Billy was third up, and he was just hoping Billy O- and Mack would get on base to let him drive in the tying run. Billy O-lined out to the SS and Mack was able to draw a walk. Now it was Billy's turn to win the game with a HR. Once again, he once again remembered his first championship game in Little Leagues where he struck out trying to hit a homer, so this time, he was determined to just meet the ball and hopefully reach a gap where Mack could score.

The first pitch sailed over the catcher's head, and Mack was off to second. Now all Billy had to do was hit a single to tie the game.

"Strike one," called the ump on a fastball that hit the corner of the plate. Billy didn't think it was even close, but when he turned to the umpire to complain, he remembered all the lessons he'd been taught about not complaining. He just shook his head, adjusted his batting gloves and stepped back into the box.

Billy recognized the next pitch as it left the pitcher's hand. It was a curve, and in a split second, he remembered when he first starting playing; his Dad throwing one curve after another in their backyard, telling Billy to watch the ball as it left his hand. Billy saw the spin. He swung.

He knew he had a HR as soon as the bat met the ball. It had that "sound." The ball cleared the right field fence, and once again, the Legends led the game 4-3. The Grasshoppers were not able to score, and the series was now going back to Lexington, with each team securing a win. With three games in Lexington, the Legends had the chance to win the entire league championship with two more wins.

The bus ride back to Lexington felt a lot shorter to everyone as they talked about the win, about Billy's HR and the chance to win the entire league, when ten weeks ago, there were in next to last place and six games under .500. The difference was that Billy joined the team.

The Royals GM had followed the team all year, and he knew the improvement in the team was directly attributed to Billy Tankersly. Not only was he leading the team in hitting, stolen bases and HRs, but he was also the cheerleader for the team, continually talking positively to the players, encouraging them. Coach Wanamaker spoke to Dillar, the Royals GM, several times during the season, reporting on Billy.

Arriving in Lexington, the Williams, including Emma, were waiting for the bus. As the players got off the bus, Emma ran up to Billy and gave him a tight hug and a kiss on the cheek. He immediately went into a full-fledged blush. The other players on the team razzed him, saying things like, "We didn't have a pretty girl kiss us for winning."

Billy laughed with everyone else, but all he wanted was a bed. The Williams saw how tired he was and loaded everyone in the car to go back to their house. As they arrived, Billy's cell phone was ringing. Billy, pulling the phone out of his pocket, wondered if it was going to be his folks, Mr. Booker or Bobby. It was Bobby.

Billy answered and heard a group of people saying congratulations all at once. It was Bobby, his Dad and Mom and Mr. Booker.

"What are you doing with Dad and Mom, Bobby?" he asked immediately.

"We are not in Kansas City or Austin, does that give you a clue?" Bobby laughed.

"No, where are you?" Billy asked with his brain going 100 mph. "Where are they?" he thought to himself.

"We are in Lexington, Billy," Bobby replied. Then Billy heard his Dad, "We know you just returned and have to be exhausted, so we'll see you in the morning. We are staying at the Hyatt Regency."

"Dad, I want to see you tonight," Billy cried out. "Tomorrow is an off day, so I don't have to go to bed right now."

Emma walked by Billy's room and overheard the conversation. Once Billy hung up, she offered to drive him to the Hyatt.

"Really, Emma?" Billy was excited that it was Emma who was taking him. He knew he would invite her in once they arrived at the hotel. He just hoped she would come.

As they drove to the Hyatt, Emma told Billy how proud she was of him. He hadn't realized that she listened to every game.

"I think you have made all the difference in the world in the team reversing from a horrible season to playing for the championship. You should hear the announcers rave about you, Billy," Emma continued.

When they got to the hotel, Billy invited Emma to come in and join his family, Mr. Booker, and Bobby.

"No Billy, this is really special for you to see your family and especially Bobby," Emma answered.

Billy said, "OK, Emma, thank you for the ride" He jumped out of the car, seeing Bobby by the front door.

He couldn't even remember the last time he'd seen his best friend, but he knew Bobby was not nearly as big as he was now.

"My gosh, you have grown a lot," Billy commented as he hugged the young man who apparently had been lifting weights.

"I've followed what you taught me, Billy," Bobby started. "I've worked harder than anyone else; I've visualized hitting a HR every time I step to the plate, but I also learned from you to cut down on my swing with two strikes."

"Are you referring to my strike-out in our first championship game together?" Billy laughed.

"Yep, you taught me, even in losing, Billy," Bobby said, with the laughter gone.

The two boys walked into the restaurant where Billy's folks and Mr. Booker were having coffee. Billy saw his Dad and started running to him.

"This is the best surprise I could ever get, Dad," Billy said in a more shrill voice than he normally used. He smiled as he hugged his Mom and Mr. Booker.

"Billy, we really don't want to keep you up too late, but how about one quick game of shuffleboard?" his Dad suggested, "and you can tell us how you are doing?"

Mr. Booker said, "You guys play. I'm tired and am going on up to the room to get some shut-eye."

Billy hugged Mr. Booker, telling him how excited he was that he had joined his folks.

Billy and Bobby played against his Dad and Mom. Billy was on the same side of the shuffleboard table as his Dad, so they got to talk a lot about baseball. At one point, he told his Dad about Emma kissing him on the check. That seemed to bring more excitement out of him than all the baseball talk, and his Dad recognized it. "Have you asked her out on a date yet?"

Billy laughed, telling his Dad "no, I'm so focused on baseball Dad that I really can't afford to think about a girl. Remember in high school when I had that crush on Abby...I lost all focus on baseball, so for now, I'm a baseball player and intend to reach the goals I've set," Billy answered his Dad about Emma, although he wasn't entirely honest as Emma did come to his mind a lot.

They played two more games of shuffleboard, changing partners, so he got to be on the same side of the table as Bobby. The competition between the two had not changed since they were kids. Bobby scored more points than Billy, which prompted one more game. This time Billy won. He was not going to let Bobby beat him twice.

Once they were done with the shuffleboard games, Billy's Dad suggested that he stay at the hotel, since the next day was an off day.

At first, Billy was a little disappointed that he would not be going back to the Williams where he could see Emma, but rooming with Bobby was far more exciting as he knew they'd stay up most the night, catching up with each other's lives and talking baseball.

Billy called the Williams to let them know he was staying at the hotel for the night. Emma answered the phone and seemed a little disappointed when he told her the news about staying at the hotel. He didn't know if he imagined it, or if she really was disappointed.

For the next four hours, Billy and Bobby talked about every game they'd each had. It was a fun night for both, and about 3:00 AM, Billy was the one that said, "We've got to get some sleep."

As Billy fell asleep, he was thinking about Ricky's record. He was going to break it.

12

Billy's First Professional Championship

Because it was an off day, Billy and Bobby both slept in but were awakened when the phone rang. It was Mack wondering if they were going to get together today. Billy explained who was here to see the championship games, Mack told Billy how fortunate he was to have his family here.

"Billy, I don't have a family to meet me, so in my mind, you are the luckiest guy on the team," Mack said.

"Well, Mack, you now have a family because I want you to join mine today as we sit and visit at the Hyatt downtown," Billy said.

Emma drove Mack to the hotel. Billy was outside waiting, hoping Emma would bring Mack over to the hotel. Once they arrived, Billy invited her to come in and meet his family along with Mack. This time, she agreed, and they all walked in together.

The day could not have been more perfect for Billy, introducing Bobby to Mack, who had become his best friend on the team. The three boys talked baseball, while Emma spent time talking to Mr. and Mrs. Tankersly. Mr. Booker joined the boys talking baseball. Billy introduced Mr. Booker as the man who taught him most everything he knew about baseball and especially about stealing bases.

"Billy, I've been following you on the radio, and I am very proud of you, son," Mr. Booker said at one point. "I have one suggestion though," Mr. Booker couldn't help but coach, even though he hadn't seen Billy play the past few weeks.

"You have not been picked off all season," Mr. Booker started.

"That tells me that you can increase the distance from first on a leadoff, and save a split second on your steals," said the man who worked with Billy for hours, teaching him how to steal a base in the first place.

"You will learn how much further off base you can get when you do get picked off," Mr. Booker finished.

Mack and Bobby were listening intently as they realized this man knew more about baseball than most they'd met.

Coach Wanamaker had called for a short workout at 3:00 PM at the Lexington Park. Billy and Mack asked Mr. Tankersly to take them to the park since everyone else wanted to at least watch the workout too. Billy's Mom rode to the park with Emma.

The workout turned out to be more listening to Mr. Wanamaker talk about the season than working out.

"Guys, I am so proud of you," he started. About fifteen minutes later, he ended with "Guys, I am so proud of you." The coach was happy, and he let the team know.

The team was ready to win a championship, and finally, Coach Wannamaker told the infielders to take their position. Out on the field, Billy was glad Bobby and his family, including Mr. Booker and Emma were there watching. He and Mack completed some slick double plays, and Billy knew his Dad was more impressed by that than any of his other plays. Finally, practice was over, and Billy and Mack joined the others to go back to the hotel. They had a nice dinner, and finally, Billy spoke up telling everyone," there's a game tomorrow." All laughed but knew Billy was ready to go back to the Williams to get a good night's sleep. Mack and Billy rode with Emma, and almost as soon they arrived, Billy was sound asleep, with his bat by his side.

When he awoke, and his mind was immediately on the game. After breakfast, Emma took Mack and Billy to the stadium. He dressed, grabbed his bat and glove and headed to the field. Infield practice was a little longer than yesterday and Billy was ready to get in the batting cage first. He drilled several balls into the outfield and felt ready for the game.

Forrest Paige was the starting pitcher for the Legends. He led his team last year in rookie ball with an ERA of under 3.00 and had done the same in Class A ball this year. The players had confidence in him.

The game started with both pitchers throwing shutout innings through the first five innings, but in the sixth inning, the visiting Grasshoppers scored a run on a single and then a double by their left fielder.

As the bottom half of the inning started, Coach Wanamaker huddled with his team in the dugout.

"OK guys, this is our inning. Let's keep the line moving," he said, with an urgency in his voice.

Leve was first up. He singled up the middle. Mack followed with another single, with Leve being held at 2B. Billy was now up with the tying run on second base, and the lead run on first base.

He watched the first pitch dart across the heart of the plate, with the ump indicating, "strike one."

Billy stepped out of the box. That had been the pitch he could have clobbered, and he took it. No more. He was swinging if the ball was even close to the plate, going back to the "contact hitting" approach he'd been taught by the coach the first day with the Legends.

Mr. Booker, up in the stands, could tell just from the sound a bat makes on contact with the ball whether it's going to be a hit or not. He could tell that Billy smashed that next pitch. Even before the ball left the park, Mr. Booker knew Billy had just hit a HR.

As Billy rounded the bases, he was looking for his folks, but he could hear Bobby and Emma screaming, "Way to go, Billy!" He wasn't about to smile as the game was far from over, but inside, Billy was smiling. As he rounded third, he saw his fan club standing and cheering. Billy felt like he was in heaven.

The game ended with Billy's homer making the difference. The Legends only had to win one more, and they would be the Class A champions.

After the game, Billy and Mack walked out together, and as usual, the Williams picked them up. This time was different. His fan club was waiting for him. Bobby couldn't stop talking about the game and Billy's homer. Mack was right there with Bobby, praising Billy for his game-winning hit.

"Billy tells me you guys have been best friends since grade school," Mack started.

"True," replied Bobby, "but it appears you and Billy are pretty close too."

With a big smile, Mack was happy Bobby wasn't jealous of the friendship he and Billy had and it was apparent to Mack why Billy liked Bobby so much. After his folks drove them to the Williams, the three boys sat on the front porch while his parents and the Williams, including Emma, were inside discussing the game, past history of Billy and Bobby, etc.

Bedtime came. Everyone left, and Billy was lying in bed thinking about the game tomorrow, not the results of today's game. He knew the Grasshoppers were throwing a left-handed pitcher who had won twelve games during the regular season. Since he batted left-handed, he would have a real challenge, but he was thinking of hitting the ball to left field each time up as he drifted off to sleep.

Game time came, and for the first time all season, Coach Wanamaker had Billy leading off.

He explained in the dugout to the team that because Billy was so fast, he felt the team could steal a run with Billy's speed, not his power. Billy was elated. He'd wanted to lead off, ever since joining the Legends, but found it strange that the coach in a championship game would make that move. He had no idea that the Royals General Manager was at the game and asked the coach to have Billy leadoff because he wanted to see as much of him as possible.

In the bottom of the first, Billy led off with a walk, promptly stealing second base on the first pitch to Mack. He took the pitch for a ball, but on the next pitch, he lined a ball to right field that sailed over the outfielder as the wind was blowing to right. Billy scored easily on Mack's double. The Legends led after only two batters.

By the ninth inning, Billy had been up four times, getting three hits plus the walk, had stolen three bases and scored three runs. Forrest was still pitching in the top of the ninth with a two-hit, shutout so far. The Legends led 5-0. The game ended 5-0 as Forrest threw his first nine-inning shutout all year. The Legends were champions of the Class A League. Billy Tankersly was voted Most Valuable Player (MVP) of the series and the celebrating was on!

Naturally, his family could not celebrate in the clubhouse with the team, but as soon as Billy and Mack walked out, there was even more cheering.

Bobby summed it up best. "Billy, get used to being on championship teams. This won't be your last," he added.

13

Arizona Fall League

Billy arrived in Phoenix one week after the championship game. He had studied up on the Arizona Fall League and found out that most of the players on the teams were the top prospects from each of the major league teams. He'd been told by Coach Wanamaker that only one Class A player from each team was allowed, so it was a great honor to even be here. But, Billy intended for it to be more than an honor; he wanted to show his skills to the scouts, and whoever else was here from the major league teams.

There were six teams, and he would be playing with top prospects from other major league organizations on his team, the Surprise Saguaros. Each major league team would choose six players from their minor leagues, and it could be Triple A players, as well as players in lower leagues.

The Surprise Saguaros had two practices before their first game. The manager, Coach Keller, was the hitting instructor for the Royal's minor leagues. Billy met him once, in Lexington, but did not know much about him, except he was with the Kansas City Royals.

At the practices, Billy found out that Skip Lawson from the Pirates organization would be starting at SS and Billy would be on the bench. He took it in stride, knowing that he'd soon get his chance.

In the two days in Phoenix, he had learned a lot about the Arizona Fall League. Coach Keller explained to the team at their first practice that last year's All-Star Game, in Minneapolis, featured sixteen AFL past players.

Coach Keller went on to share that nearly sixty percent of all AFL players make a major league roster, with one hundred All-Stars over the years.

"Therefore, guys, this is your chance to really shine. You have been chosen by your major league team to be here because they think you have what it takes to reach the majors, and yet, only six out of ten of you will achieve that," the coach told the team. "My job is to do my best to make sure that all of you are in the six that make it," concluded the coach.

Billy had never heard so many instructions being given to players as they took batting and infield practice.

"Do this, don't do that" seem to be what Billy was hearing, but he paid special attention to the "do this" comments from the coaches. There were two other coaches on the team. One was the Triple A manager for the Royals, the team Billy had set a goal of reaching by his eighteenth birthday. He wished he was going to be starting.

They would be playing for seven weeks, so he was hoping he'd get to start some of the games. For now, he watched the team win their first game with Skip Lawson, the other SS on the team, getting two hits. Skip played in Triple A last year, and Billy knew the Pirates were planning on giving him a shot at the bigs next year. That meant that Skip would probably get most of the starts.

When Coach Keller announced the starting lineup for the second game, Billy learned he was not only starting but leading off.

The game began with the grandstands completely packed. Obviously, the people out here wanted to see top prospects who might be in the majors next year. Billy had set goals of playing Double A ball his second year but seeing many of these players who were already playing Double A made him wonder if he could even make a Double A team.

As he stepped into the box in the first inning, he immediately called timeout, and stepped out, making sure he was focused on this game, this at bat and this pitch. The first pitch was a curve, and again, Billy thought of his dad throwing one curve after another that first year. He was ready for it and hit a scorching line drive into the right-field corner. As he dug for second, he knew he had a double where he didn't even have to slide.

On the first pitch to the second batter, John Temple the RF from the Texas Rangers, Billy was able to see the catcher give the sign and immediately, Billy touched his cap. This was a signal that he and John went over before the inning started, just in case the situation came up. John knew to expect a fastball, and he rifled it to left center, enabling Billy to score easily.

Billy had two hits and one stolen base before the coach pulled him, putting Skip in to play the last four innings. Billy watched Skip him like a hawk, wanting to learn from a SS, who was almost ready for the majors. He noticed how he played certain hitters a different way. In between innings, Billy asked Skip how he knew to change where he was playing on the field.

"Billy, I've studied every one of their players. I did this before getting here so I would know where to play them. Jack Jacobs, their big centerfielder for example, never hits to the opposite field, so I played him pretty much right behind the bag at 2B," added Skip.

"Wow, I thought I studied everything, but you've definitely taught me I've got a long way to go," said Billy in amazement.

The remaining seven weeks flew by with Billy wishing there had been another seven weeks. The team won their division and was playing for the AFL championship.

Billy was shocked when Coach Keller announced the starting lineup. He was starting at SS and batting leadoff again. He'd started more than half the games over the seven weeks but knew that the Pirates wanted to see their prize SS in this championship game. Unfortunately for Skip, Billy was hitting .386, and led the AFL with fourteen stolen bases. Keeping him out of the starting lineup was almost impossible.

As Billy stepped into the batter's box, he'd already made up his mind to take the first pitch, just to see what the pitcher would throw. Billy knew the pitcher was an up and coming starter for the St. Louis Cardinals but during the seven weeks, Billy had not seen him pitch.

"Strike one," indicated the home plate umpire. With one pitch, Billy had seen enough to know this was probably the best pitcher he'd ever faced. The pitcher threw a changeup on the first pitch, letting Billy know this was one confident pitcher. He knew not to guess on the pitches, but to follow the ball from the time it left his hand and be ready for anything.

With the count, 2-2, Billy lashed a line drive to left field, rounding first thinking it might have been in the gap between the fielders, but putting the brakes on as he saw the ball was being thrown to 2B.

John Temple was batting second again, and the coach gave him the bunt sign. Instead of letting Billy steal second, he was giving John the bunt sign, indicating he wanted John to sacrifice Billy to second. The dugout applauded, as John laid down a perfect sacrifice bunt. Billy was on second with one out. Tracy Schwartz was next up. He was a 1B from the Oakland organization and played Double A ball the past year. Tracy had some power, so Billy was ready to get a jump on any hit and score the first run. All of a sudden, the pitcher turned and tried to pick Billy off second. Billy dove back to the bag but wasn't sure if he was safe or not.

"Safe!" roared the ump with his arms stretched out, indicating Billy had made it back. But in his first year of professional baseball, this was the closest he'd come to being picked off. He remembered what Mr. Booker told him about needing to get picked off so he could learn even more about a pitcher's pickoff move, but right now, Billy was just thankful this had not been the game he would "learn."

On the pitch, Tracy hit a slow ground ball to the third baseman, and Billy remembered scoring his first run for the Legends on a slow ground just like this when he'd been on second. This time, the third basement looked at Billy, daring him to run, before throwing a zinger to first base to get Tracy out.

Spooks Garfield, the catcher was next up. For a catcher, he had good speed plus power. Billy looked in from second to try to get the sign from the catcher. But, the catcher gave about five signs, and Billy had no idea what the pitch would be so he could not help Spooks with what was coming his way. It was a fastball that Spooks took for a strike. Billy looked to his third base coach to see if there was any way he'd give him the steal sign. Yes, there it was. His hand touched his belt and then ran across his chest, and back down to his belt again. That was the steal sign. Billy took off as soon as the pitcher glanced at him and then back to the plate. He was probably not expecting a steal of third base this early in the game with one out. Billy's speed took everyone off guard, and when the catcher saw what was happening, he tried to hurry the throw, and it bounced off the third baseman. Billy slid in with a bent knee slide, which meant he was up and running as soon as the ball bounced off the third baseman. He slid into home plate in plenty of time to score the first run.

With only one out in the first inning, the Saguaros had the lead and never trailed the rest of the game. Billy had two more hits, two more stolen bases, and two runs. Defensively, he made two excellent plays to his right, where he threw while jumping in the air. Both throws were like darts going across the diamond. Overall, Billy felt the Royals had to be impressed with his first Arizona Fall League experience. He ended up hitting .350 over the seven weeks and stole eleven bases. His first year of professional baseball was now behind him.

14

Home For The Winter

Billy was exhausted, and all he could think about was sleep. It felt good to sleep in his own bed. Once lying down, his mind raced over the past summer and fall. As tired as he was, he could not go to sleep as one thought about a game would bring another thought. He finally got to sleep, but the next morning, he was still exhausted. Mrs. Tankersly called to Billy asking if he wanted breakfast, and he rolled over yelling at her, "No Mom, I just want to sleep." And sleep he did. Twelve hours of sleep. By the time he got up, it was almost 2:00 PM.

His Mom was working on a project of some kind, and Billy asked if she would mind if he went over to Mr. Booker's. She said, "not at all, but be home for dinner." He smiled, thinking how good that sounded after being away from home so long.

Billy ran over to Mr. Booker's, excited to talk about his first professional season with his longtime coach. He knocked twice, and finally, Mr. Booker came to the door.

"Holy Smokes," he exclaimed. "A professional baseball player at my door. OK, tell me all about your season."

"Mr. Booker, I had a great first season, much to my surprise," began Billy. "When I saw how good the guys were on our team and other teams, I must admit I got a little scared."

"Why would you be surprised, Billy?" Mr. Booker interjected.

"I guess I just didn't realize how much natural talent I had. Once I accepted that, I started playing really well," Billy answered. "It made me work even harder, that's for sure."

Billy spent the rest the afternoon telling Mr. Booker about his accomplishments, about other players on the team, especially about his new best friend, Mack. He explained how the travel got to him. He told Mr. Booker that his goal of breaking Ricky Henderson's stolen base record was still his goal, but he realized how much harder that was going to be than when he first imagined it.

"Do you know how many years Ricky played?" Billy asked the only groundskeeper ever elected to the Hall of Fame.

"Unlike you, Ricky wasn't drafted until the fourth round. It took him three years to reach the majors so his first full season was in 1979 and he played for 24 years," the coach answered. "He only played in 89 games his first season, but then averaged close to 140 games a season until his last two seasons. In fact, he only stole two bases his last season and eight the year before." Mr. Booker said, explaining to Billy that his speed slowed as he aged.

"He still stole 1406 bases," Billy laughed. It was the first time he laughed since getting home.

"Hey, I've got an idea, Billy," the coach announced as he stood up. "Let's go up to the academy and see how fast you can run to first base."

"I'll have to get my spikes," Billy laughed, thinking this was his first day of his off-season, and here he was running again.

As Mr. Booker stopped the car in front of his home. Billy ran in, told his Mom where he was going, got his spikes and was back in the car with Mr. Booker in about 30 seconds.

At the Academy, Billy said hi to everyone, and then he and Mr. Booker went to the field that was just an infield. With Mr. Booker standing on first with the same stopwatch that Billy had seen every year since he was a kid. He loosened up and then told his coach he was ready. He was timed on the first run at 4.1 seconds.

"Billy, you can do better than that," Mr. Booker encouraged him, knowing that 4.1 for a left-handed batter was above average in the major leagues.

Billy knew he'd been timed at 3.8 once while with the Legends, so he made up his mind to get to first at least that fast.

Mr. Booker said, "go" and Billy was off. He knew this time was faster.

"Good job, Billy, you broke 4.0, but just barely, and I know you can do better than that," Billy's longtime coach encouraged him.

"Do you know how fast Billy Hamilton was timed last year, Billy?" Mr. Booker asked.

"No," Billy answered.

"He was timed at 3.3 seconds," Mr. Booker said. He then added that the scouts that timed him had various times, all less than 3.4 seconds though. "Think you can reach that mark, Billy?"

Billy was determined to break 3.5 seconds this afternoon, but 3.7 secs was his best time.

After an hour at the Academy, Billy was exhausted but determined to hit 3.3 or at least, 3.4 before Spring Training.

The rest of the winter seemed to fly by for Billy, with him spending most of his time on the exercise equipment in his basement or at the Academy. He was building up strength. One of the things Mr. Booker explained to Billy was that Ricky Henderson had 3,055 total hits, so to break his stolen base record, Billy was going to have to hit at least .280 once he reached the majors. That meant he had to get stronger, not just to hit, but to last 24 years. All winter long, he kept thinking about how hard it would be to play that long in the majors. It made him conscious of the fact that he had to be in the best shape, year around. There would be no off-season for Billy Tankersly.

At his seventeenth birthday party that included his parents and Mr. Booker, his Mom handed Billy an envelope that had come in the mail that day. On the front was the Kansas City Royals emblem. He tore it open as fast as he could and read out loud that he was being invited to the Royals Spring Training. Everything else was forgotten. He was going to Spring Training with the Royals. Learning about it this way was a memory Billy would never forget. Sharing the excitement with the people he loved was a lifetime memory.

Billy knew that very few Class A ball players are invited to the major league Spring Training camps and the chance of making a major league roster was about 1 in 1000 if that. But the fact he had been invited gave him a bit of extra confidence, and a chance to turn some heads with how good he was.

Mr. Booker worked out with him pretty much every day, giving Billy advice on hitting, stealing, and defense. Billy thought Mr. Booker knew more than any coach he would ever have. He pulled stats out of his head like that was all he ever did. He explained to Billy that even though he had been invited to the major league camp for Spring Training that by the end of the first week or two, he would probably be assigned to a minor league camp.

He then explained to Billy that the minor league spring training camp was harder than the major league camp. For example, they had to be at the park at 7:15 AM every morning, which meant they would have to catch the bus from the motel by 6:00 AM.

Once at the ballpark, Mr. Booker continued, the players would eat breakfast, suit up and be ready to hit the batting cages at 7:50 AM. By 9:00 AM, the players would be divided into four groups, Triple A players in one group, Double A in another, High A and Low A in the final groups.

Mr. Booker was preparing Billy for what was ahead for him. He told Billy that he had no insight, but expected Billy to be sent to the Double A group since he'd played last year in the High A group.

"Normally, Billy," the coach continued, "the General Manager of the Majors makes the decision, and they almost always start a player in a camp for the next level up. It's then up to the player to show that he can play ball at that level or he will be sent to the lower camp within a couple of weeks," he concluded.

The weather had warmed up enough in Kansas City that Billy ran outside in a park close to his house for a couple of weeks, with Mr. Booker by his side most days. They would go to the Academy in the afternoons, and Mr. Booker would time Billy from home to first base. The former groundskeeper pushed the 17-year old to reach a time of 3.7 seconds to first base before Billy had to leave for Spring Training. On the last day, the goal was finally reached with Billy being timed at 3.6 seconds. That gave him even more confidence in showing off his speed at the Spring Training camp.

"Billy, if you don't mind, I would love to come out to Phoenix to watch you in Spring Training," Mr. Booker said to Billy, not in a questioning way, but a matter of fact manner that indicated he was coming, no matter what.

The next day, he and Mr. Booker arrived at the airport two hours ahead of time. It had been all over the news that when flying out of the Kansas City airport, you needed to be there two hours before your flight. Billy wondered why so early as they got through the gate an hour and thirty minutes before the flight. That gave Mr. Booker more time to school Billy in what Spring Training was going to be like. Even though he would probably be the youngest at the major league camp, Billy intended to make an impression with his speed and hitting. Mr. Booker explained on the plane that Billy's passion was going to take many lumps along the way, but the secret was to never give up.

"Coach, is it ever easy for anyone to play in the majors on natural talent, or does it take the amount of work you've laid out for me?" Billy asked.

"Talent by itself is worthless, Billy," the coach started. "There's a place in the Bible that says it best. Faith without action is useless," Mr. Booker told him. "In other words, everyone who makes the majors does have talent, but it takes any player, no matter the talent, working his butt off constantly to reach and stay in the majors."

"I will remember that, Mr. Booker," said Billy. "You have been such a good coach for me that I want to break Ricky's record for you; to show you that I have listened to you over all these years," said the young pupil who was eager to learn. Billy was going to have a good Spring Training. He knew it.

The plane landed right on schedule, and the Royals had a car waiting to take them to the hotel. Mr. Booker found out ahead of time where the team would be staying and booked himself into the same hotel, so he asked if he could bum a ride.

"Absolutely, Mr. B," the driver said.

Billy was shocked that the driver knew him from many years ago.

"How you doing, Fishhook?" Mr. Booker asked.

"I'm still hanging out around baseball, just doing whatever I can, same as usual," the man replied.

Then he turned to Billy and said, "Billy Tankersly, our number one pick last year. Son, you had better kick butt and get up to the bigs fast. We need you," Fishook encouraged the young player.

Billy smiled and watched the big city lights of Phoenix disappear and finally, the sign that said, "Hyatt Place" appeared.

They checked in, ate a snack, and Billy headed to bed. He wanted to be up far earlier than usual, so he'd be wide awake for his first day of Spring Training.

15

Billy's First Spring Training

Seventeen years old and getting to attend the Kansas City Royals major league Spring Training didn't go exactly as Billy had anticipated. He caught the bus, but there were only five other players on it. All were pitchers or catchers. As Billy chatted with them on the way to the park, he learned the position players wouldn't be there for another four days.

He wondered why he'd been invited to arrive before the position players. He was soon to find out.

Getting off the bus, Hall of Famer Brett Dumont greeted him. Billy was shocked as Brett said, "Hi Billy. If you're wondering why you are here with the pitchers and catchers, it's because I asked to have you come early so I could work with you," the famous 3B said.

"Really, Mr. Dumont?" Billy said out loud. Just then, Brett turned to say hi to Mr. Booker.

"How you doing, Mr. B?" Brett asked.

"Hey Brett, let's put it this way, I can still outrun you," laughed Mr. Booker.

Billy watched them hug each other and realized that Mr. Booker was genuinely liked by everyone he came in contact with. He hoped someday he could greet people with the same respect these men showed for each other.

"Billy, let's you and me go chat for a little while," Brett Dumont said to the stunned young man.

As they walked to Brett's office, he explained to Billy that the Royals had a lot of money tied up in him. He was an investment in the organization.

Therefore, Billy was going to get three extra days of training before the position players arrived.

"First, Billy," Mr. Dumont began. "Mr. B told me your goal is to break Ricky's stolen base record, but there is no way you can do that without concentrating on your hitting," Billy's new instructor began. "But there is one thing even before hitting," Brett stated. "Do you know what it is?" he asked Billy.

"Hard work," Billy replied.

"Before that, Billy. You have to understand the word attitude. The dictionary says that attitude is the same as outlook. Playing baseball is one of the hardest occupations there is to maintain your attitude because, by the nature of the game, you fail more than you succeed," continued Brett. "So how do you keep your attitude positive?" Brett asked Billy.

"I don't know," responded the 17 year old. Billy thought Mr. Dumont would be asking him about his stance at the plate, or keeping his swing level, or something about hitting. But no, the Hall of Famer was asking him about attitude.

"Billy, here is the secret. You always look forward, remembering you are a number one draft pick out of all the players drafted last year. You would not have been selected by the Royals if they did not see you as a person, before seeing you as a player," Brett continued. "It was your character that attracted the Royals to you in the first place, which was about five years ago. We know any player being considered for a number one pick has to have talent, but we saw something different in you. We saw a young boy who sacrificed just about everything to become better. We saw a boy who struck out in a championship game, who did not let it affect his performance the next year. We saw a kid who worked with Mr. Booker every chance he had. And Mr. Booker kept us informed on how you were doing, not just in stats, but in your attitude," Mr. Dumont paused for a breath.

Here was the Hall of Fame 3B giving Billy insight into why the Royals drafted him in the first round and advice on how to improve even more.

"Billy, this is a hard game," Brett continued. "Keeping your attitude up during slumps is almost impossible, but what isn't impossible is to learn how to shorten the slumps. The way you do that is to come to each game, slump or not, visualizing getting hits. Remember, for you to break Ricky's record, you need to have at least at least 3000 hits. Not many achieve that alone. But, Ricky had 3,055 hits to reach his 1,406 stolen bases. So as fast as you are, you have to focus on hitting all Spring Training, all year, and all your career," Mr. Dumont informed Billy.

"I started visualizing when I first started to play baseball. My Dad talked to me over and over about visualizing what I wanted. He told me that I would make at least two outs for every three times at bat. I remember thinking that he was wrong. I was going to get two hits every game," Billy laughed.

"Mr. Booker told me that several years ago, Billy, so I already knew. What you don't know is how good the pitching is as you progress up the ladder. The pitching in the major leagues is something like you've never seen before. You are going to have slumps like you've never dreamed. But understand what I'm saying to you. You do not have to have long slumps. You can shorten them, just because of your attitude. Never get wrapped up in your last game. Remember attitude is your outlook. Do whatever you have to do to keep looking forward and not backward," Brett concluded his first lesson with Billy.

Mr. Dumont dismissed Billy from his office, telling him that Coach Abrams was outside waiting for him. Billy left the meeting with Mr. Dumont and met Coach Abrams, who showed to the clubhouse, telling him to suit up.

Out on the field, the coach then called all the pitchers together and told them that they had a live batter to pitch to if they wished. Several volunteered and before he knew it, Billy was in the cage, but with a catcher behind him and a live pitcher on the mound.

Billy was about to hit against a major league pitcher, even if it was Spring Training, and the pitchers hadn't warmed up, which meant they were going to be warming up against Billy. The first pitch came in, and Billy let the pitch go by. Just then, he realized that John Gordon was the pitcher throwing batting practice. Gordon had won twelve games for the Royals last year and was considered their third starting pitcher in the rotation.

Gordon threw another fastball and Billy hit a line drive to right field. He was feeling good and swung at Gordon's next pitch. It was a changeup that had to be 20 mph slower than the pitch before. Billy swung at it, as it bounced on the plate. Gordon smiled at the youngster, knowing the kid had never seen a changeup drop a foot before hitting the plate.

"Hey, Billy," said the catcher, who Billy did not recognize. "you need to realize that pitchers in the majors have all sorts of pitches you've probably never seen before. Keep your eye on the ball as it leaves the pitchers hands," he continued.

Billy remembered the long days in his yard playing with his Dad and facing one curve after another, but never a changeup that seemed to drop like Gordon's last pitch. He remembered his dad preaching to him about watching the ball leave the pitcher's hand.

"OK," Billy said to the catcher. "Have him throw another one."

Billy watched the pitcher, and as he released the ball, he saw the spin. It was a curveball with that much spin he thought. Again, Billy swung and missed. He realized that the spin did not automatically mean a curve was coming his way. It had more to do with how much spin.

"One more time," Billy asked the catcher to have Gordon throw it again.

This time, Billy saw there was no spin on the ball. It looked like a four-seam fastball, and in a split second, before the ball reached the plate, Billy swung. The ball cleared the center field fence.

"I thought you were going to have him throw me a curve ball," Billy turned to the catcher.

Nick Simmons, the catcher, laughed and told Billy that no one in the majors had ever asked for a specific pitch, and if they did, you could be certain they would not get that pitch. Gordon wasn't about to give Billy another curve, but now he wished he had, as he was still admiring the power Billy showed on the last pitch.

Without another word, Billy knew the next pitch would be a curve or that changeup he'd seen two pitches ago. He watched the ball spin, and this time saw it drop, but it was still over the plate, and Billy slashed a line drive to left field.

Billy smiled to himself. He had hit a home run off a major league pitcher and then hit his curve the opposite way. The rest of the day, Billy took more batting practice and some infield practice with pitchers hitting to him. Then he played a game of pepper with five pitchers and catchers standing about 15 feet from him. They would throw him a slow pitch and the object was to hit each ball to a different player. They insisted that he call out who he was hitting the ball toward. It was a lot harder than he imagined, but the purpose was to teach him how to read the infield and outfield and hit the ball where he saw holes. This pepper game helped him with his bat control.

When the day was over, he dressed and joined Mr. Booker in the grandstands.

"How'd I do, Mr. Booker?" Billy asked naturally. It seemed he always wanted the admiration of others but was such a good listener that he took the criticism just like the admiration.

"Billy, you had a great workout," the Hall of Famer answered. They are looking for five tool individuals, and you showed off each of your five tools today. Your speed is better than most. You have a strong arm in throwing. Your range at SS is above average, and your hitting for average is excellent as is your power. The game has advanced so much that team's look for more than the 'five-tool player' as they did in the past though. The sixth tool is character. They want positive leaders in the clubhouse. I don't think this is a surprise to you, but you score high on all the 'six' tools," Mr. Booker told Billy.

The bus was waiting for the pitchers and catchers to finish their workouts, so Mr. Booker suggested they ride back to the motel in the car he rented.

Billy's answer surprised and impressed the former Hall of Fame Groundskeeper.

"No, Mr. Booker, I should ride back on the bus with the guys who may end up being teammates of mine," Billy responded.

Mr. Booker left with Billy sitting in the stands waiting for the bus, with the very few remaining people who came to the practice session. It never dawned on Billy that these were probably all scouts.

16

Billy Assigned To The Double A Camp

On the bus back, Billy got to know several of the other players. John Gordon was the first pitcher who threw to Billy, so they got to know each other better on the return trip to the hotel.

Back at the hotel, several of the guys went to the bar to have a drink, but obviously, Billy was underage, so he went to his room to review the entire day.

The next two days were the same for Billy. He intended to show management that he was fully capable of moving up the ladder. He would prove himself worthy of being called up to the Royals after September when the baseball clubs could increase their rosters.

Spring Training did not go precisely as Billy planned, and by the eighth day, he was reassigned to the Double A camp. Now he had to show that he could, at least, play Double-A ball.

He was really getting into the grove of hitting Double-A pitching, it was time to break camps and start the regular season.

Billy knew that the first baseman, Mike Kessler, would be one of those called up in the September call-up. As he studied the rest of the team, he was pretty sure that Mack would be called up, since he'd made the jump from the Double-A team to the Northwest Arkansas Naturals along with Billy. Another player who Billy felt was an exceptional player was the center fielder, Amos Trotter. Billy felt the closest these four players to as the team started working out at the Arvest stadium, one that the

Royals had built for the Northwest Arkansas Naturals with a seating capacity of 6500. It was a good park to hit homers as the foul lines, both in left and right field, were 325 feet from home plate.

The Naturals played 70 games at home, which meant Billy wanted to know every square inch of the ballpark before the season started. He checked the infield, the outfield, the fences and even how far it was from the SS position to the grandstands. If there was a popup that the third baseman was not able to get to, he wanted to be able to outrun the ball and catch it as it came down at the grandstands, or even in the first row of seats. He had the coach time him from his SS position to the first row of grandstand seats that jutted in between third base and the outfield. Everything was put in his memory because he wanted nothing more than to win a championship for the Naturals and be called up to the bigs in September.

The first game of the season was against the Corpus Christie Hooks, the Double-A team for the Houston Astros. Billy started hot. He had three hits, and drove in two and stole two bases. The rest of the series proceeded to go the same way. After three games, Billy was leading the league in about every category listed. His defense had saved two runs, and he was leading the league in that category.

"How could things be better?" he said to Bobby on Skype. The two boys who grew up together were skyping each other two to three times a week whenever their schedules let them. Billy had Bobby's travel team's schedule with him at all times.

"Billy, you're going to get called up before September if you keep playing like in the series against Corpus. I've even gone to some of the Corpus games

Metal Spikes II

because they are only about two hours from where we live. Last year, they didn't finish very high, but they had some special players on their team. I'm pretty sure that one or two are on the Astros roster right now," Bobby rattled off this particular night.

Billy thought he was really blessed to have such a good friend. Bobby knew him better than any of his teammates ever would.

By the time, the team reached the halfway mark, they led the league by two games, and Billy was the up and coming star. He was elected to the All-Star team after batting .328, hitting 15 HRs and stealing 34 bases. He led the league in all those categories, plus he had driven in 40 runs, hitting from the leadoff position.

17

A Sudden Surprise

Before the second half of the season started, Billy was called into the coach's office, just like he had been last year. It had been good news last year, so maybe this would be good news too, he hoped as he knocked at the door with the sign, "Manager's Office."

"Come on in, Billy," Coach Abrams said, with a smile on his face.

"The Royals GM just called me, and you are being promoted to the Triple A Omaha Storm Chasers," said a man who was almost as proud of Billy's promotion, as he was. "You are to catch the first plane out to Omaha."

Billy left Coach Abrams' office, not having a clue what to do about telling his current teammates, many which he'd built a good bond. It was an off-day because of the All-Star break, and none of his teammates were around. He wondered if they'd even believe him if they were with him. In truth, he knew they would. Billy had a first half of the season not many had achieved.

At the airport, Billy was shocked to see Mack.

"What are you doing here?" he asked as the boys hugged each other.

"I've been promoted to the Storm Chasers, Billy."

"Me too!" Billy chimed in. He wondered why Coach Abrams had not told him about Mack's promotion, but this was going to be fantastic, he thought, playing with Mack at Triple A.

Just like in the first half of the season with the Legends, the boys sat next to each other, only this time, not on a rattley bus, but in an airplane to Omaha, Nebraska. They would be playing in the Pacific Coast League that had 16 teams. One of the teams, the Round Rock Express, was in Austin, Texas, which meant Bobby could come out to the game to see him play. He told Mack all about Bobby. While talking to Mack, he realized he hadn't talked to Bobby recently. He hoped he had been drafted.

The flight didn't seem to take long, and before they realized it, they were landing in Omaha, Nebraska. They knew the Storm Chasers were at home this week. They hoped someone would be at the airport to give them some directions.

As they were coming down the escalator to get their luggage, a man was holding up a sign that said, "Billy and Mack."

After getting their luggage, the man drove them to the Hyatt Place in Omaha. He explained that they needed to be at the ballpark by 9:00 AM and they would be guided from there. Once Billy was in his room, he connected to the Internet to learn more about the Storm Chasers. He found out that the stadium was named Werner Park. There wasn't an explanation, and Billy wondered who this Werner guy was? Then he checked attendance records for the league so he could anticipate the size of the crowd he'd be playing for. He learned it was around 5,000, but what interested him the most was the fact that the Round Rock Express drew the highest attendance in the league and it was more than 8,000 a game. After learning as much as he could, he took his bat and laid down on his bed. It must have been comfortable because when his 6:00 AM alarm went off, he was surprised the bat was in bed with him. He had actually gotten out of the habit of sleeping with his bat, but when rolling out of bed, he hit his knee on it, and if anyone had been in the room with him, they would not have known if Billy was crying or laughing. After turning the light on, he realized this might be the best day of his life, even if his knee was still hurting. But first, he had to Skype Bobby.

"Hey Billy," Bobby answered. "I'm sorry I haven't called you recently," Bobby began. He continued in his rapid-fire words that always painted a picture if you listened intently. If you didn't, you'd never be able to understand Bobby. He definitely had not picked up a southern drawl.

"Billy, I got drafted by the Royals in the sixth round," Bobby exclaimed. I'm currently in the rookie league and already have three HR's," Bobby spoke, with so much excitement in his voice it was hard for Billy to get in a word edge-wise. Finally, there was a break. Billy figured it was just so Bobby could get a breath, but it was a chance for Billy to jump in and tell Bobby what had happened to him.

"Bobby, "I was just promoted to the Storm Chasers and am in Omaha right now," Billy told his best friend.

"What?" Bobby shouted into his headset. "You have been promoted to Triple A, and you're just 17 years old," Bobby said, almost to himself.

"Yeah, it surprised me too, but I had an excellent first half with the Naturals, and getting promoted didn't surprise me as much as maybe it should have. At least, I led the league in stolen bases," Billy laughed. "And I think the Naturals will win the championship in Double-A, but if I play good enough to stay up here, I won't get to be a part of it," Billy confessed to himself, only it was a comment to Bobby.

"Gag me, Billy," Bobby laughed. "I think I will be shocked if you don't break Ricky's stolen base record. That's been your goal since we were in T-ball," Bobby continued, laughing.

"Yep, Bobby, that's a goal I intend to reach. I've worked hard, followed many coach's advice since those T-ball days and have really learned a lot about stealing. It's not as simple as it looks," Billy continued.

"Neither is hitting a home run," Bobby interrupted, which Billy knew would happen. He laughed to himself.

"Oh, I forgot to tell you, Bobby, I also led the league in home runs," Billy couldn't resist telling his best bud.

"Come on, Billy. Did you really?" Bobby asked.

"Yep, I've really learned a lot in pro ball. I've had some of the best coaches in baseball teach me things I never realized."

"OK, tell me about your team."

Billy heard how Bobby felt he was getting good coaching as well. He told him that he had focused on his power, and each of his coaches had helped him. He said that each time he came up, he was expecting to hit a homer. Billy was impressed with Bobby's attitude and knew he would someday be on the Royals with Billy. That was exciting.

The boys hung up, and Billy hurriedly ate breakfast. He finished just in time to get on the bus to the ballpark.

George Keller, the manager of the Storm Chasers, greeted Billy and Mack as they entered the clubhouse. Billy knew Coach Keller from the Arizona Fall League.

"Welcome to the Storm Chasers," Coach Keller said in his first breath and then added, "you guys will be sitting on the bench initially, so get used to it," he concluded.

Billy looked at Mack, and they both had the same expression. If the coach had seen their looks, he would have realized they both thought, "Why did you bring us up here if we are going to sit on the bench?"

18

The Storm Chasers

The game was the first in a three-game series against the Nashville Sound, who were 3 ½ games ahead of the Chasers in the standings. Billy and Mack were on the bench just as the coach had told them. Both questioned why they were even brought up. The game was lopsided as the Chasers scored four runs in the first inning and Nashville never caught them. The final score was 6-4, but there was really no chance for Billy or Bobby to get in the game, even as a pinch runner, which Billy was sort of expecting. "Mack, I'll bet we get in tomorrow's game," Billy told his friend. "I just have a feeling that both of us will start."

"I'd be stunned if that happened, but like you've preached to me, if you don't believe, it won't happen. So, I'll start visualizing both of us starting, just like you will be doing, Billy," said Mack, laughing. He knew Billy was right, so he went to sleep that night, picturing he and Billy in the starting lineup.

Lo and behold, when Coach Keller posted the starting lineups, Billy was starting at SS, hitting eighth, and Mack was starting at 2B, hitting seventh.

Mack grounded out his first time up, and Billy struck out. The young 17-year old didn't keep that memory in his head. Out in the field, he visualized hitting a line drive to center his next time up. His visualizing stopped when the first ground ball came his way. It was far to his right. Alec Apollo, the third baseman, tried to get it but was not able to get to it in time. Billy was able to backhand it in short left field. In one motion, he caught the ball, twisted in the air as he rifled his throw to Ted Barns, the first baseman, who came close to doing the splits, stretching for the ball.

"Yrrrr Out," roared the umpire.

The crowd loved it and gave Billy a standing ovation.

"Wow, with support like that, we need to win the division," thought Billy.

The game turned out to be a rain-shortened game, but because it was stopped in the sixth inning, it went down as a Storm Chaser win. Billy got on base before the rain started, and promptly got the sign to steal. He'd been watching the Nashville pitcher closely and knew exactly when to break for second. He slid in a good second before the ball arrived.

"Safe," indicated the umpire. Billy had his first stolen base in Triple A. He wished they'd save balls for special occasions, like a first steal. He laughed to himself, realizing it wasn't the first steal that was important, but the last steal, which he knew would be a record far surpassing Ricky Henderson.

As he dressed in the locker room after the game, Arturo Cruz, the left fielder whose locker was next to Billy's said, "Nice hit and steal, Billy."

"Hey thanks, Arturo. You made a great catch in the third inning, preventing them from scoring two more runs," responded Billy.

"You want to get a bite to eat?" asked Arturo.

"Sure, can Mack join us?" Billy responded, not wanting to leave Mack out.

"Absolutely," the left fielder replied.

The three young players found a restaurant close by, called Amitos. As they ate their Mexican food, they discussed other players on the team, the standings, and who Arturo expected to be called up in September.

"I'm pretty sure Ted Barns, our first baseman will be called up. Also, Jorge Fostomia, our catcher should be called up, as the Royals catcher is in the last year of his contract and will be a free agent next year. Other than those two, plus me of course, I don't think any others will get called up," Arturo laughed.

"Well, add me, and Mack to your list, Arturo," Billy laughed back at him.

Billy and Mack learned that many of the players didn't speak much English, so it was nice sitting with Arturo who had learned the English language well in his three years of being in the states.

"Where are you from, Arturo?" asked Mack.

"San Luis Potosi, which is fairly close to Monterrey. We are close enough to Mexico City and Guadalajara that I got to watch a lot of baseball growing up. We have amateur fields in Mexico that are better than those in America because next to Soccer, baseball is the national sport of Mexico," answered Arturo.

He continued, "Many of the players on our team and the Royals speak Spanish. Most know enough English to know what you are saying, but they may not know how to respond in English."

"It was sort of that way in Double-A, Arturo," Billy added. He was happy that the Mexican kids got to play baseball and become good enough to play Triple A or in the majors. He wished more American kids would play baseball instead of football or basketball. Just as he silently thought that to himself, he decided he was going to put some of his baseball earnings back into whatever city he was playing in, for more modern parks. He thought every young kid could learn more about how to be successful in life if they just played a few years of amateur baseball.

The boys ate their dinner and returned to the Hyatt Place hotel. Billy read the sports news of the day and almost fell asleep with his laptop on his lap. He turned it off, rolled over and started thinking about tomorrow's game. He wondered if he would start again. He wondered if he'd be called up in September. He wondered about so many things that he was having a hard time getting to sleep. Finally, he got up, turned his laptop back on to see if there was any news about the rookie league. He wanted to see Bobby's stats. Before finding a site to get that information, he was sound asleep, this time with the laptop on his lap and his bat on the right side of the bed.

The next day, Billy found himself and Mack in the starting lineup again. They were definitely getting their chance.

Mack singled his first time up, walked his second time up and grounded out to third his last time up. He was happy going 1-2. Billy singled his first time up and stole second base. He was surprised to get the steal sign when he was on 2B, but he judged the pitcher's motion and took off as soon as his foot passed the rubber. The coaches realized something that Billy was not aware of. The Royals GM had been following Billy all season and wanted him to be tested at Omaha. He slid into third and was surprised to find the catcher hadn't even thrown the ball.

Billy thought to himself, "safe by a mile" as he stood up and dusted himself off.

Felipe Gomez, the right fielder, followed up with a single to right field, allowing Billy to score the first run of the game.

The game seemed to be over before it started in Billy's mind, but he realized he'd stolen four bases in his second game at Triple A. He did not think that was a record, but he was sure to get the attention of the Royals. He had three hits, with one being a double off the right-field wall. He thought it was going to be his first home run at Omaha, but the wind held it up, and Billy had to hustle to get to second. He slid in on the inside of the bag reaching out with his right hand to grab a corner of the base. When the umpire yelled, "safe," Billy was thankful because he had not hustled out of the batter's box thinking it was a home run. That fact did not get by Coach Keller.

After the game, Coach Keller said he wanted to see Billy in his office. All the other times, when called to the manager's office, he had received good news. He expected the same today after stealing four bases.

"Billy, you will never reach the majors with a stunt like you pulled today," Coach Keller began. Billy's optimism stopped in a heartbeat.

"You did not hustle out of the box on your double," the coach continued. Do you realize you were the potential winning run?" the coach asked.

"I know it turned out that way Coach, but I did not think about it at the time," Billy answered.

"There was no thinking about it, Billy. You did not hustle out of the box," said Coach Keller, in a not so kind way.

"I assure you, Billy, if I were to report to the Royals about that, there would be no chance of you being called up," the coach continued. "I won't write it in my report today, but I never want to see that happen again, is that understood?" Coach Keller said, looking into Billy's eyes.

"Yes Sir, it will not happen again," Billy replied.

He was dismissed from the Manager's office, got dressed and went back to the hotel by himself. He wondered if he'd get to start in the next game, which was against the Oklahoma City Dodgers, a farm club of the Dodgers. The Dodgers were one game ahead of the Storm Chasers and were leading the division. If Omaha could win this series, they would stand a great chance of winning the division and playing in the playoffs for the Triple A championship.

Billy thought back to the Naturals, wondering if they won their division. He questioned himself about why he had not checked on the Internet to see how the Naturals were playing without Mack and him. The Storm Chasers were playing a night game, so Billy had the time to catch up on the Naturals. He found a site that was for Double-A and saw that the Naturals had won the division and were now playing for the Double-A championship. He called Mack, and the two boys met in a restaurant close by and discussed their days with the Naturals, and now with the Storm Chasers. They wondered together if one or both of them would be called up in September.

19

A Big Surprise

Arriving at Werner Park field, Billy saw that both he and Mack were in the starting lineup again, only this time, he was batting fifth, with Mack sixth. To Billy, being moved up in the lineup in just his third game with the Storm Chasers was a big deal, and especially in a series against the Dodgers.

"Hey Billy," Mack called out. We've both been moved up in the lineups."

"Congrats, Mack," Billy answered, but he was thinking about hitting fifth, and how that might change his approach in each at-bat. He was going over the lineup in his head, "Aturo and Enrique are leading off and batting second. Alec and Ted are hitting third and fourth, so if two of them get on, I'll get to bat in the first inning and be able to drive in runs," he continued thinking.

His thinking was stopped as they played the National Anthem. All the players on both sidelines stood, with the caps over their hearts. Billy thought that was pretty nice, considering many of the players were from Mexico or another Latin American Country. At the end of the anthem, the crowd yelled, "Play ball" and the Storm Chasers ran out onto the field to an enormous cheer from the fans.

Johy Tripoz was on the mound for the Storm Chasers. He was considered the number two man in the rotation, but he had the lowest ERA among the starting pitchers. It was an incredible 2.37 in sixteen starts, so the team felt good in this first game of the series.

"Strike one!" yelled the ump as the game began. Johy had started the game with a 96 mph fastball on the outside corner to the right-handed batter. Then he saw the coach motioning Billy to move closer to second base than the other hitters. He wondered how the coaches could look at specific stats and tell him exactly where to play.

"I've got it," he heard Mack call out on the popup the leadoff hitter for the Dodgers had hit sky high. When it finally came down, Mack was camped under it just behind the bag at second.

The next two batters struck out, and Johy was looking good after half an inning. The team knew how important it was to score in the first inning to give Johy a little leeway.

Arturo led off with a single, and Enrique followed with a sacrifice bunt to get Arturo to second. He laid down a perfect bunt that the Dodger's pitcher fielded and then threw wild to first base. There was no way the first basemen could reach it as it bounced into the dugout.

"Automatic second base," yelled the umpire at first base. Then he added, "The first base runner has to stay at 3B."

Billy was in the dugout with two thoughts, "What a great start for the team behind the pitching of Johy, now they needed to score these two baserunners, and this means I will get up in the first inning."

Alec struck out on three pitches, so it was Ted's turn to drive in two runs, with Billy next up. The Dodger coach signaled to the catcher to walk Ted initially. With a new rule this year, the pitcher did not have to throw four pitches but just indicated he wanted the batter to walk.

That meant that Billy was coming up with the bases loaded in the first inning of a crucial game for the Storm Chasers. A win here would tie his team with the Dodgers for first place in the division. Apparently, the Dodger's manager wanted their pitcher to face the 17-year-old rookie, rather than Ted who led the team in HRs.

"Ball one!" bellowed the umpire. Billy was a little surprised the pitcher threw him a curve on the first pitch, but he watched it all the way and knew it was inches inside and low. With a 1-0 count, he expected a fastball. The radar gun showed it was a 95 mph fastball and Billy just watched it cross the plate.

"Strike one," called the ump. Billy stepped out of the box. He did not wear gloves like many of the players did, but he still fidgeted with the bat, as if he had gloves on. Stepping back into the batter's box, Billy was guessing he was going to get another curve. He was not even thinking of hitting a grand slam home run, but just doing something to get one or two runs in. He knew that would be enough for Johy.

"Strike two," called the umpire on a curve that hit the outside of the plate. Billy watched it, thinking it was going to be a ball, but could not argue with the ump because the ball probably hit the corner he thought.

Now a 1-2 count. He was in the hole, and the pitcher could now throw whatever pitch he thought the batter might swing at, but definitely off the plate. Billy let another curve go by without swinging. It dropped almost to Billy's feet, and even though it looked good leaving the pitcher's hand, Billy knew exactly what the ball was going to do, by the spin he saw on the ball.

The count was now even, 2-2. Billy could hear the encouraging cheers from the Storm Chasers dugout. However, it was a voice from the stands that caught Billy's attention. It was Emma!

Billy stepped out of the box, looking into the stands. About four rows back, behind the Storm Chasers dugout, sat the entire Williams family, Mr. Booker, and Billy's Dad and Mom. Billy tipped his hat to them with a smile on his face as he stepped back into the batter's box.

Billy started to swing at the next pitch but held up his swing and the umpire called "Ball three." The catcher motioned to the third base umpire to see if Billy had struck out. The umpire at 3B gave the safe sign with his arms extended. So the count was 3-2, with the bases loaded. Billy had a chance to make the Royals take note, but more importantly, he had an opportunity to help the Storm Chasers take the lead in the first inning.

It was a fastball straight over the plate. Billy swung and actually saw the ball hit his bat. It felt solid and sounded the same. The ball had hit the sweet part of Billy's bat and according to one scout at the game had an exit speed of 108 mph. Billy ran before he looked up to see the ball clear the RF fence. He did not know whether to smile, cheer or just trot around the bases with no expression, but he couldn't help waving his arms in the air.

The fans were cheering so loudly, Billy could not hear what the third base coach said as he hit the bag on his way to the plate. Half the team was at the plate waiting for Billy, including Mack who was next up. Chest bumps, special handshakes and someone taking his helmet off, and messing up his hair were part of the celebration. But, it was only the first inning, and there was an entire game in front of them. The guys that met Billy at the plate returned to the dugout except for Mack who was in the batter's box. He stepped into a first-pitch fastball and drove a line drive to the gap between left field and center. It was a standup double. The Storm Chasers dugout was as loud as Billy had ever heard it.

Jorge and Felipe struck out, and Mack was stranded at 2B, but the Storm Chasers led, 4-0 on Billy's grand slam.

Johy did not allow a hit in the second and third innings, but in the fourth, the right fielder for the Dodgers hit one almost precisely where Billy's homer had landed. However, there was no one on base, so the solo home run left the score 4-1 as Billy came up in the bottom of the fourth.

Again, he watched a first-pitch curve.

"Ball one!" shouted the ump.

Billy hit the next pitch as solid as the pitch in the first inning. But this time, it was a line drive directly at the second baseman. He hit it so hard; he was barely out of the batter's box when he saw the ump waving his hand in the air, indicating Billy was out.

Mack and Jorge hit ground balls to the SS who threw both players out easily. After four innings, the Storm Chasers maintained their lead and Johy was pitching great. The Dodgers only had one hit, the solo homer off the starting pitcher for the Storm Chasers.

Johy was still pitching in the eighth inning, which was the longest he had gone all year. Billy looked at the scoreboard to see he had thrown 89 pitches so far.

"We're behind you, Johy, let them hit a pitch or two," yelled Billy from his position. Johy turned to

Billy and with a smile, tipped his hat. He knew that the Storm Chasers had the best defense in the league and Billy and Mack had made it stronger since being called up.

The first pitch was hit directly at Billy, one of those hits that can handcuff a player, but Billy fielded it cleanly and threw to Ted for the first out of the inning. Then Johy got a little wild, walking the second batter on four pitches and then walking the third batter on a 3-2 count. He now had thrown 99 pitches, and Coach Keller walked to the mound slowly. He knew what he was going to do and as soon as he reached the mound, he waved his left hand in the air, indicating he wanted Guma Gomez to relieve Johy. Guma was a sly lefty who threw mostly curves of one kind or another.

On Guma's first pitch, a sharp ground ball was hit over second. Billy was fast in reaching the ball and flipping it behind his back to Mack, who completed the double play with a great throw to Ted. The fans were going wild, and no one noticed Guma tipping his hat to Billy and Mack for a sensational double play.

Billy led off the bottom of the eighth with a single to right field. Everyone in the stands knew Billy was going to steal. Every one of the Dodgers knew the same. No one knew which pitch. Mack looked to the third base coach for a sign. Billy glared at the coach as well. Both were expecting a "take" sign along with a steal sign for Billy.

They got it. Billy took his usual lead and took off for second base as soon as the pitcher's foot crossed the rubber. He didn't look back but only toward second base. He watched the second baseman for signs if it was going to be close. He could tell it was.

Billy dove for the outside of the bag, reaching out with his left hand as far as he could stretch. He waited. "Safe," yelled the umpire. "No way," the Dodgers second basemen yelled back at the umpire. The Dodger manager came running out to second base telling the umpire he was wrong and to check with another umpire.

"I don't need help, Tim," yelled the umpire back at the manager whose face was red with emotion.

"Come on, ump, that wasn't even close," screamed the Dodger manager, face to face with the umpire.

Billy just stood on second base, listening to the argument, but knowing no matter how much they argued, he was safe.

After about two minutes of the manager yelling, the umpire yanked his hand in the air meaning he was kicking the manager out of the game. That only brought on more yelling, but eventually, he walked away kicking dust as he passed 3B.

The Dodger pitcher who had come in the last inning in relief was not used to this kind of interruption, but he was throwing the ball back and forth with the catcher while they argued. He had pitched 33 games during the regular season so far. He wasn't fazed by Billy stealing second and immediately enticed Mack to strike out on a changeup that only reached 79 mph on the scoreboard radar. Jorge hit a popup on the infield, and Enrique struck out, leaving Billy stranded at 2B.

The game ended a short while later with no other hits for either team, and the Storm Chasers tied the Dodgers for the North Division lead.

Billy dressed and hurried out to the parking lot, knowing Emma and the entire crew would be there. He was surprised to think of Emma first.

20

Emma

As Billy walked to the parking lot, he saw Emma running toward him, and before he knew it, she planted a big kiss on his cheek while hugging him.

"Hey Billy, you were great, nearly shouted Emma, with a big smile as she stepped away and looked into Billy's eyes. For the first time, he noticed she had beautiful brown eyes.

They laughed, and Billy hugged his Dad next. It was so good to see him. Then he gave his Mom a big hug thanking her for coming up to Omaha. Mr. Booker looked at Billy, thinking, "This kid's lost some weight this season." Mr. and Mrs. Williams were not far behind in hugging Billy, and telling him what a great game he played.

They wanted to take him out to dinner, and for some reason, he didn't even think about inviting Mack to join them. All he could think about was the kiss Emma planted on his check.

They got in the van Billy had ridden in many times as his folks took him from one game to another in the little league and traveling baseball seasons. Billy and Emma were in the back seat, which was the third row. He didn't know why but he found himself reaching for Emma's hand. She didn't pull away, so they rode to the restaurant holding hands in the back seat while the adults in the front talked about the game. Every now and then, Billy heard his name, but he couldn't get his mind off how nice Emma's hand felt in his.

Over dinner, Billy told all of them what had happened in their games, what he had done, and intended to do. Billy's Dad was surprised when he told him that his goal was to be called up in September.

"Already? Billy, keep in mind you are still only 17 years old. I doubt if a 17-year-old has ever been called, except someone like Bob Feller or someone back in that era," said Mr. Tankersly.

"Well, I've got my goal. I'm doing everything just the way you and Mr. Booker taught me," smiled Billy.

Dinner was over, and on the way back, again Billy reached out and held Emma's hand in the back of the van. Billy was not thinking about baseball.

He knew the Williams and his folks were staying for the entire three-game series, so he was hoping he'd get to see Emma again, but his Mom's advice two years ago about Abby turned out to be right, as she would have taken his mind off his goal. His Mom's words echoed through his mind. "Billy, if you get serious with Abby, you might end up with your mind on Abby and not baseball. Are you sure that's what you want?" she asked.

Billy went to sleep trying to get his mind off Emma and back onto baseball. He realized his Mom might have really been giving him good advice that he should heed right now. However, it wasn't as easy as it was two years ago in telling Abby he couldn't see her anymore.

The alarm went off, and Billy's mind was on baseball. He did not even think about Emma until he was getting dressed for the game.

"Hey Billy, where did you go last night?" Mack asked.

"My folks and Mr. Booker are in town with the Williams," Billy replied. "We went out to eat dinner." "Well, why didn't you find me and invite me to go?" Mack asked.

"Mack, I should have. I'm really sorry, but maybe you can join us tonight if they take me out again." Billy explained.

"Was Emma with them, Billy?" Mack asked.

"Yes, she came up with her Mom and Dad," Billy answered, thinking, "Did Emma flirt with Mack too?"

At that point, Coach Keller came in to post the starting lineup, and also to talk to the team.

"Guys, we are now tied with the Dodgers for first place in the division. We've got 20 games left so we cannot afford a letdown," said the coach. Before anyone could answer, Coach Keller, started laughing saying, "OK, I know none of you ever thinks about losing, so let's go out and whip their butts, today and tomorrow."

The team cheered like a high school team might. These guys wanted nothing more than a championship.

As the Storm Chasers took the field, Billy looked up to the stands to see where they were all seated today. He saw Emma before seeing his folks, Mr. Booker and the Williams. His mind was back on her.

21

Game Two of The Series

He realized it must have looked funny, but he turned around facing the outfield, and slapped his own face a couple of times saying, "Baseball Billy, Baseball,"

Mack saw him and inched over toward Billy saying, "What was that all about, Billy?"

"Just me trying to focus on the game," Billy replied like there was nothing more than him preparing himself for the game.

"OK, let's get 'em," yelled Mack.

Ace Gurruara was the starting pitcher for the Storm Chasers, and he'd been one of the bright spots all season, according to Arturo.

"Let's get 'em," Billy yelled to Ace right before the first pitch.

Apparently, he didn't need Billy's encouraging yell as he struck out the team on 12 pitches, which meant he'd only thrown three balls off the plate in this first inning. Billy hoped that continued.

Coach Keller told Billy before the game that he was going to be leading off today. It was a surprise to Billy, but one he relished. He would get a chance to have more at-bats and consequently, more opportunities to steal when he got on base.

Billy heard Emma's voice, yelling for him to get a hit. He lost his focus for a split second, but a split second in baseball separates the greats from all the others. In that period, a fastball cut the inside of the plate, and the ump yelled, "Strike One."

He was focused on the pitcher now, and for some strange reason, he could not hear Emma or anyone else in the grandstands. The pitcher for the Dodgers got his sign and started his windup. Billy saw the spin on the ball. It had a tight spin that meant it would drop at the last minute. Billy waited until the last moment, and then, slashed a ball down the third base line that was inside the bag. He was running. The left fielder picked it up cleanly and rifled a throw to second. Billy had rounded first and thought he could get a double. The ball and Billy arrived at almost the same moment at 2B. Billy dove in head first, and once again, grabbing the bag as he slid past it.

"Safe," yelled the umpire.

Billy was surprised as he felt the second baseman had tagged him a brief second before he got to the base. The second baseman felt the same and immediately started arguing with the umpire. Their manager came out but was not about to be tossed from this game, so he put up a mild argument and went back to the dugout.

Billy was on 2B with a double.

The first pitch to Alec, who was batting second was a fastball across the center of the plate. Alec took the pitch, probably wishing he'd swung as the next two pitches were great sliders. Billy was tempted to steal third on the last pitch but guessed it would be a fastball. It was another slider over the plate. "Strike Two," bellowed the umpire.

"There is definitely a difference between Double A and Triple A pitching," he thought to himself.

Just then, Emma once again, unannounced, popped into his brain. In that brief second, Alec hit a sharp ground ball at the Dodgers shortstop. Billy was caught off second. The SS saw Billy hesitate and immediately threw to the second baseman rather than to first. Billy broke for third but saw the ball there ahead of him, so he turned and raced back to second base. It was only the second rundown Billy had been involved in. He knew if he could keep the third baseman and second baseman throwing the ball back and forth but not being able to tag him, it could give Alec a chance to get to second, but only if he could make the Dodgers throw to the third baseman to get him.

The radio announcers were having a great time telling their audience about how long Billy kept the Dodgers from tagging him out.

"I've never seen a rundown last this long," one announcer would say only to hear the other announcer say, "He's headed to third!" They are going to finally get him now. No, the Dodgers threw it away. Billy Tankersly is going to be safe at third, and Alec Cruz is safe at second," the announcers excitedly told their audience.

Billy was exhausted. He had never been in a rundown that long. He was amazed he was still safe and had not created an out for the team. He knew he had been napping, thinking about Emma after his double.

Standing on the third base bag, dusting himself off, he also knew the Storm Chasers had an excellent chance to take the lead in this game two of the series. Enrique Williams was up to bat, and if he hit a fly ball to the outfield, Billy knew he could score on any of the outfielders. He was no longer thinking about Emma.

Enrique knew his job was to hit the ball, at least to the OF, to get a sacrifice fly. He knew Billy could score on just about any outfielder even if they were charging in on a short fly ball.

Billy watched the pitcher as close as ever. If he tried to throw a slider or tight curve that might get away from the catcher, Billy was ready to run. Enrique hit the pitch to deep centerfield, and Billy ended up scoring easily with Alec getting to third. Ted Barns followed with a double to get Mack home, and the Storm Chasers led 2-0 in the first inning. Mack and Jorge followed with groundball outs, so after one inning, the Storm Chasers were optimistic with Ace on the mound.

Ace Gurruara was pitching his best game of the season. After seven innings, the score was still 2-0. Billy had grounded out and flied out his next two times up. He was disappointed that he did not get a chance to steal a base, but thought, "the way Ace is pitching, I might not need to even get up again." He knew he would get one more chance in the bottom of the ninth if the Dodgers scored two runs, and he definitely did not want that to happen.

While in the dugout when Jorge was up, Mack came up to Billy, and asked, "Do you realize that Ace is throwing a no-hitter?"

Billy just turned away. No one was to say it out loud. If a pitcher was fortunate enough to carry a no-hitter into the last two or three innings, it was bad luck for anyone to talk about it. The pitcher would even sit alone so no one could speak to him about it. It was an unspoken rule that Mack apparently didn't know.

Finally, Billy turned back to Mack, sitting him down, and whispering, "Mack, you are not supposed to say it out loud." It was like a lightbulb went off in Mack's brain, and he replied, "I knew that Billy. Whoops, sorry."

The first batter in the top of the eighth for the Dodgers grounded out to Mack who made a nice play close to second base. The next Dodger hitter lofted a fly ball to shallow centerfield, which Enrique caught with ease. Billy looked at the scoreboard. Four more outs for Ace to have his first no-hitter. This was a time to stay focused.

Ace struck the next batter out, and going into the bottom of the eighth, hitting for the Storm Chasers would be Jorge, Terrace Itzebar, and Felipe, who had made two beautiful catches in centerfield.

The Dodger pitcher was Slim Tyson, who was known to be the best closer in the league. The Dodgers were going all out to get a win, bringing him with the Dodgers on the short end of the 2-0 score. He lived up to his expectations striking all three Storm Chasers out. Billy wasn't going to get a chance to bat again if Ace could just get three more outs.

The ball was thrown around the infield, and you could feel the pressure. Not just with the infielders, but with the outfielders and the fans in the grandstands. "How could Ace seem so calm while warming up," Billy thought, as the ump said, "Play ball."

"Strike one," everyone in the stands could hear, as the entire stadium was deathly quiet. Everyone knew what was at stake.

Ace looked in, got his sign, and threw an 81 mph change-up that left the Dodger's batter dumbfounded. He'd been expecting a fastball and looked foolish with a half-hearted swing. What would Ace throw him next?

Billy was trying to get Jorge's sign that he was giving Ace, but Jorge had his legs closed like there was a runner at second base. Billy heard the crack of the bat and instinctively dove to his right. He felt the ball hit his glove hard as he hit the dirt. Billy watched the ump raise his right arm into the air, thankful he'd been able to react that fast. Ace tipped his hat to Billy.

The next batter hit a popup behind second base, and Mack smothered it. "Two outs," he shouted to the outfielders.

Billy's mind was not on Emma. It was not on his double. It was on every pitch. "No way were the Dodgers going to break up Ace's no-hitter if there was a ball hit to his side of the infield," he thought.

On the first pitch, the next batter hit a long fly ball toward center field. The announcers were calling it a home run. Felipe was having no part of that. He leaped at the fence, with his glove actually over the fence. He not only saved a run, but he also saved a no-hitter, and the team didn't know whether to jump on him or Ace. Ace was closest, and the team piled on him. Ace had just pitched his first no-hitter, and the Storm Chasers were now in first place, all alone.

<u>22</u>

Storm Chaser Lead Expands

Billy and Mack ate with Billy's parents, the Williams and Mr. Booker. Emma sat next to Billy, but she was sitting between Mack and him. Billy felt uneasy, knowing or at least thinking that Emma had flirted with Mack the same as she had with him.

Mr. Booker complimented Billy and Mack on the two double plays they had made.

"Mack, I think you've helped improve Billy," commented Mr. Booker. "He seems to be quicker in getting the ball out of his glove and throwing it."

"Mr. Booker, Billy and I have spent many hours on non-game days just working on our double plays. I think Billy has helped me," Mack responded.

"I would imagine that's true, Mack. Hopefully, the two of you will be playing for the Royals in the not too distant future," the former groundskeeper replied.

"When do players get called up?" Billy asked.

"September first, but you have to be on their 40-man roster, and neither of you boys are on that," Mr. Booker explained.

You will be starting your playoffs very soon for the Pacific Coast Champion, and ultimately the Triple A championship if you get that far. Durham won it last year," he further explained to all at the table.

Mack was impressed that Mr. Booker knew just about everything about baseball, about the minor leagues and majors.

"Were you a groundskeeper in the minors, Mr. Booker?" Mack asked.

"Yes, Mack," Billy said. "Mr. Booker had to work his way up. He's shared many of the stories about the minors back in his day. But, he kept at it, and after nine years, he made it to the Royals. He is the only groundskeeper voted into the Hall of Fame. He helped so many rookies coming up, no one ever forgot, and when it came time to vote for players in the Hall, one of the Hall members brought up Mr. Booker. He was so well liked, and respected, he ended up getting the 10th highest votes ever for induction", continued Billy.

Mr. Booker interrupted Billy. "Bottom line, Mack, I was a great groundskeeper, the greatest, " laughed Mr. Booker. He continued, "The truth is I love this sport, and being able to be around young men like Billy, gives me great joy."

Billy's Mom spoke up. "We've seen it first hand, watching you help Billy over the years , so it's no wonder you got voted in. You have been my inspiration in starting my new business."

Billy knew his Mom had been working on a project but had no idea she had her own business.

"Business is just like baseball, in many ways," added the Hall of Fame Groundskeeper. "You certainly have to accept what a batter in baseball learns fast; you fail a lot, but you have to constantly face the next day with optimism," he smiled.

Dinner ended, and they all walked to the car. Billy and Mack got in the back seat with Emma sitting between the two boys. No one said a word. It was like they were all wanting to say something, but everything seemed so boring compared with the question on both boys minds.

"Was Emma flirting with me, or Mack?" Billy was thinking. His mind was off the game entirely. Emma had his focus for the moment, but he still could not think of a thing to say.

Arriving at their home, Billy and Mack sat on the front porch alone for more than an hour discussing the situation with Emma and the third game of the series coming up. They knew that neither of them was on the 40-man roster so they would not be called up in September.

As far as Emma, Mack told Billy that she had never flirted with him. He had flirted with her a lot, but she never returned his advances. Mack was a year older, so Billy just accepted the fact that he'd flirted with Emma for two years, while in Lexington. He was relieved, but now he questioned in his mind if she was going to get in the way of him reaching the majors.

That night before getting in bed, Billy actually prayed. He was not sure if it was a prayer, or if he was just talking into the air, but he asked God to help keep his mind on his goal, and not to let anything get in the way.

The next series started with the Storm Chasers winning the first two games. The third game was a tight game, but the Storm Chasers pulled it out in the last of the ninth and won 2-1. They now had a two-game lead that they hoped to maintain the rest of the season.

September first came, and four of the Storm Chasers were called up to the Royals. Billy was not one of them. The season continued for the Storm Chasers trying to win, not just the Northern Division Championship, but also the entire Minor League championship.

Billy kept hitting and stealing bases. When the regular season for the Storm Chasers ended, Billy was leading the team in stolen bases while hitting .314. He also led the team in walks and runs scored. The manager, Coach Keller, brought Billy into his office after the last game of the regular season.

"Billy, I want you to know something. About the middle of August, the Royals put you on their 40- man roster. They did not see a need to tell you at that time because they had no intention of bringing you up on September first," said Billy's manager. "I'm telling you now, because Skip Anderson, the Royals SS got hurt yesterday. He is day to day, which means they do not know how bad his injury is, and it may be one day or ten. But you need to be at least aware, there is an outside chance that you might get called up," added Coach Keller.

"Holy smokes," thought Billy. His heart was beating 100 mph. "I've got to call Bobby."

Before Bobby could even say hello, Billy said," Bobby, you will never believe, I'm on the Royals 40-man roster and could be called up!"

"No frickin' way, Billy," Bobby was almost as excited as Billy.

"What do you mean you might get called up, Billy?" Bobby asked.

"Well, Coach Keller told me that around the middle of August, the Royals put me on their 40-man roster. I didn't know that until tonight. No one told me. Coach said that they were not bringing me up September first, so there was no need to tell me," Billy continued.

"So why is he telling you now?" Bobby asked.

"Well, apparently, Skip Anderson, the SS for the Royals, got hurt yesterday and they don't know how badly," Billy answered.

"If it's bad, does that mean you will be playing on the Royals during the playoffs?" Billy asked, in amazement.

"Gezzzz, Bobby, I don't know, but I have chills thinking about it," Billy said. He added, "I haven't even asked about you, Bobby. What's up with your first season as a pro?"

"I've been promoted," Bobby answered. "I'm playing for the Lexington Legends now,"

"Really, who are you staying with?" Billy asked, hoping it wasn't the Williams.

"A really nice family that you stayed with earlier," Billy answered.

"The Williams?" Billy almost shouted into the phone.

"Yes," Bobby shouted back, not really knowing why they were shouting.

"Have you met Emma?" Billy asked.

"Sure, Billy, she lives here too," Bobby answered with a question mark in his voice.

"Well, obviously, I'm not dating her, but sure would like to, when the season is over," Billy replied, hoping his best friend would say, "I won't date her, Billy."

"That's funny because I've been thinking the same, just wondering how to approach her since she is a year older than us," Bobby laughed.

"Hey, I saw her first," Billy laughed but wasn't really laughing inside. He was jealous. That was a new emotion for him. He'd never had a girl to be jealous over, but his stomach was churning with nerves, excitement, and jealousy. He was surprised at his reaction.

"Billy, don't worry. Unless she likes HR hitters over stolen base leaders, you've got no worries," Bobby laughed again.

Billy wondered if his best friend was just kidding him, or being serious. It really didn't matter. He had a chance to be playing for the Royals.

"Bobby, if you want to date Emma, go ahead. Heck, I'm going to be playing for the Royals while you waste your time away with a girl," Billy shot back with his mind back on baseball.

"No way, Billy Tankersly. I'm going to be on the Royals with you next year," Bobby said defiantly.

Both boys laughed and decided to get off Skype and keep their minds on baseball.

"Billy, I'll be watching, and hope Anderson isn't hurt too bad but I'm glad you are being considered," Bobby closed.

23

Division Playoffs

With the Storm Chasers winning the Northern Division, their first game was going to be against the Memphis Redbirds, the Triple A club of the St. Louis Cardinals, who won the Southern Division. The Redbirds had the better record during the regular season, so they were the home team in the best of five series. The Storm Chasers had a day off before the series was to begin. Several of the Storm Chasers were going to see Elvis Presley's Graceland Estate. Billy decided to join Mack, Felipe, Enrique, and Ted. They all pitched in for a cab ride to Graceland.

On the way, Enrique brought up Felipe's catch in Ace's no-hitter.

"Felipe, I've got to ask; what were your first thoughts when you realized you saved Ace's no-hitter?"

"Oh my gosh, there were a million thoughts in my head," gushed Felipe. "I was happy to have saved Ace's no-hitter, but even more than that, I was thankful that God gave me the speed to reach the fence in the first place," Felipe replied, sort of laughing.

"You thanked God," Billy laughed. While you were still dangling over the fence."

"I thank God for most things, Billy," Felipe started off, sounding like he was preaching.

"I read the Bible daily, say prayers every night, and believes God answers them. Remember when you got hurt, Ted?" Felipe asked.

Ted had been sort of quiet, unlike his usual self, and when he heard the statement from Felipe, it brought back the memory of when he'd hurt his back in early August. The doctors told him he would be out for at least two weeks, but he showed up to the ballpark the next day and played.

"You really prayed for me, Felipe?" Ted asked.

"The very moment they carted you off the field," said Felipe.

"Wow, that is really strange. Because after the doctors told me two weeks, I expected to be put on the DL where I would be out for at least two weeks. But I also prayed that I could play the next day, and by the morning, my back didn't hurt at all," Ted said, surprised that Felipe had prayed for him too.

Billy listened intently to the conversation.

"Do you guys pray all the time?' he asked.

"Well, Billy, if you have a relationship with God, it's more like just talking to Him, knowing he hears you," Ted answered first.

Felipe asked, "Billy, have you given your life to the Lord?"

"Yes, back in traveling baseball, I got hurt really badly in Emporia, Kansas at a tournament. The doctors told me I could be out for weeks or months, but not to expect a miracle," Billy told his teammates about his experience in the hospital.

"I prayed for a miracle that night," Billy continued. "The next morning the doctor came in and told me it wasn't as bad as first thought, and I'd be playing again within a week."

"From that point on, when I really needed something, or someone else did, I've prayed, but not very often," Billy added.

"You'd do yourself a service by reading the Book of John completely, studying the attitude of Jesus," Felipe piped in.

"Why that book and why Jesus?" Billy asked, not having gone to church as a kid, and not really understanding anything about his prayers other than to talk to someone invisible and wondered why he was even "praying." When he asked himself that question, he always remembered the doctor coming in not long after he prayed, telling him his injury wasn't as severe as he first thought.

The cab ride to Graceland was almost over, but Billy hoped someone could explain to him something about Jesus and the Bible.

"Billy, come to church with me next week, and that might answer your question," Ted spoke up as they were getting out of the cab.

"I will," yelled Billy as Ted was already standing at the fence around Graceland.

The boys toured Elvis Presley's home. He'd heard some of Elvis's records, but he died long before Billy was even born.

After the tour, back in the cab, the boys started singing "Jailhouse Rock," after hearing it at Graceland. They laughed and laughed. It was a relaxing afternoon away from baseball. It would be hard for anyone else to understand the rigors of traveling all the time to play the game they loved. Today was good for all the guys.

Back at the hotel, Billy went to the room he was sharing with Mack. Mack stayed downstairs with the others, and that gave Billy time to think and prepare for the first game of the Pacific Coast Championship.

Billy knew the Redbirds would be throwing their best pitcher in the first game. His name was Zack

Hudson, and he had the lowest ERA in the PCL. It was a record for the league as he pitched 33 games and had an ERA of 1.96. Billy knew for sure he would be playing for the Cardinals next year.

The game started under a bright blue sky, with the temperature in Memphis at 68 degrees. Perfect baseball weather Billy thought as he stepped into the batter's box to start the series.

On the first pitch, a fastball hitting 97 on the radar gun, Billy lined a shot to the gap between right field and center. On same days, against some teams, Billy would have stretched his hit into a double. But against the Redbirds with Justin Hart in center and Jake Bean in right, he knew he'd be thrown out at 2B.

Mack was hitting second, and Billy looked to the third base coach to see if he was being given the steal sign, but instead, the coach was signaling for Mack to lay down a sacrifice bunt to get Billy to second. Billy wondered, "has the coach lost confidence in me being able to steal?"

Mack fouled off the first pitch. Billy had been running because he didn't want their pitcher to pick up Mack's bunt and fire to second base before Billy got there. Back at first, he looked to third for the steal sign. He didn't expect to get it with an 0-1 count on Mack. He was shocked to see the coach's hands cross the letters of his uniform and his left hand then touching his left leg, and all this after he'd touched his hat, chest, arms and about every other part of his body, so the Redbirds could not pick up the sign.

Hudson looked over to first, but not for long. He knew Billy would not be stealing with an 0-1 count on the batter.

But Billy was off like he had jets in his metal spikes. He slid in, far ahead of the tag. Billy thought "why did I even slide?"

On the next pitch, Mack sent a ground ball past the third baseman, but Billy had to pause to make sure the SS didn't get the ball and catch him off second. The ball skipped off the SS's glove, and Billy was off for third. Mack didn't stop at first base but headed to second as the left fielder was recovering the ball off the shortstop's glove. The play was in front of Billy who did not get a good jump off second, but when he saw the ball go into short left field, and the fielder throwing to second, Billy rounded third with no intention of stopping.

The second baseman saw what was happening and as soon as he got the ball from the left fielder, he planted his feet and threw a strike to the catcher. Billy slid past the plate grabbing a corner with his left hand.

"Out," yelled the umpire while Billy was still laying on the ground. He knew he was out, but was hoping the manager would ask for another umpire's advice, but no such luck. He was out and headed to the dugout with Mack on second and one out now.

Enrique flied out to right field, and Mack advanced to third, but now, there were two outs. Ted hit a sharp ground to the shortstop who immediately threw him out. Billy's out at the plate cost them a run as he could have scored on Enrique's fly to right field.

The Redbirds scored three runs off Jose Gonzales in the first inning and going into the top of the fourth, Billy was leading off again, hoping he could redeem himself from being thrown out at the plate.

He took a couple of pitches, both curves outside and called balls. So with a 2-0 count, Billy figured he was getting a fastball, and drilled his second hit to right field. He looked for the steal sign with Mack up at bat. He got it. Taking a six-foot lead, Hudson immediately tried a pickoff, with Billy diving to the bag, knowing he was safe. Hudson held the ball a long time before finally delivering a pitch to Mack. Billy was off and slid into second base safely. Mack eventually walked, and Enrique took Hudson to a 3-2 pitch. Billy and Mack were both running, but Enrique took ball four to load the bases, as the pitch was outside.

The manager of the Redbirds came out to the mound and patted Hudson on the back while waving his hand for the RHer, Ben James. James took his warmups, and Billy and Mack talked between second and third.

"Knocking Hudson out this early is great news, Billy," spoke Mack to Billy.

"I'm not so sure. Heck, I had two hits off Hudson," Billy replied laughing.

James was ready, and his first pitch to Ted was another ball outside. Obviously, none of the Storm Chasers were going to be swinging unless they got their pitch.

Ted got it on the next pitch, and he clobbered it. He hit it about 30 feet past the center field wall, for his second grand slam of the season. The score was now 4-3, in favor of the Storm Chasers.

Gonzales hadn't given up a hit since the first inning, and the bottom of the fourth was no different. Two strikeouts and a hard grounder to Mack's left, who scooped it up and fired to Ted for the third out.

Neither team scored in the fifth. The top of the sixth, Jose got a little wild, and Coach Keller walked to the mound slowly after the first batter walked. This was a playoff game, and neither manager was going to leave their starters in if they got in any trouble at all. Typically, when the manager walks to the mound, he already has his mind made up to bring in a reliever, but the manager said a couple of words and walked back to the dugout.

That seemed to get Jose back on track, and he struck out three straight batters to end the top of the sixth.

Billy was up second in the sixth, and he sliced a ball down the third base line. He thought he had another hit, but apparently, the third baseman made a great play because Billy saw the ball hit the first baseman's glove at the same time he hit the bag. "Tie goes to the runner," he thought.

"You're out," the first base umpire roared.

Billy was not happy at all. He said, "Are you sure?" facing the ump. "You want to argue young man?" the ump replied. Billy could tell from the tone of his voice, it would do no good to argue or even say another word.

Mack flied out to center to end the inning. The score going into the top of the seventh remained 4-3.

That was the way the game ended with the Storm Chasers winning the first of the five-game series. Billy did not get up again but was just happy the Storm Chasers won the first game.

Over the next three days, the Storm Chasers won two more games to win the Pacific Coast America Division. Billy had a total of 10 hits and four stolen bases in the three games. Now it was time for the

Triple A Championship, to be played against the Reno Aces, who won the Pacific Coast Pacific Division.

24

Triple A Championship

Reno had two of the best pitchers in minor league baseball, but one had been called up by their parent organization, the Arizona Diamondbacks. That meant the Storm Chasers would only have to face one outstanding pitcher as the remaining staff was hittable. The series started in Reno as they also had a better record than Omaha.

Game one went as expected. Don Gibbons, the pitcher for Reno, limited Omaha to two hits over the first seven innings, while Reno had scored five runs off Jose Gonzales, who started for the Storm Chasers. Billy did not have one of the hits as he had gone 0-3 but had a chance to get up to bat in the seventh if one runner reached base.

Gibbons had thrown 87 pitches coming into the top of the seventh, far more than his usual. Many of his pitches had been fouled off by the Omaha players, but no one had even walked.

DH Terrace Itzebar was first up and on the first pitch lined a ball to deep left field that landed at the base of the wall. Terrace ended up on 2B as the left fielder had trouble picking the ball up.

Arturo was next up. He had been put down in the batting order because of a month-long slump. He had only three hits the past month, and his average had sunk to beneath the Mendoza line, which meant below .200.

He swung at the first pitch and missed the curve by a good six inches. Gibbons was making most of the Omaha team look foolish, but on the next pitch,

Arturo laid down a perfect bunt down the third baseline that Reno had not been expecting with Omaha trailing by five runs. Arturo reached first long before the throw. Now there was a man on first and second and no outs.

Jorge, the catcher, was up, with Billy in the "on deck" circle. Jorge took a called first strike but then held off on three straight curves that missed the strike zone by quite a bit. The pitching coach for Reno came out to talk to Gibbons. Apparently, he was tired. All the while, the pitching coach was talking to Gibbons; the reliever in the bullpen was warming up fast.

The umpire came out to break up the discussion, with the pitching coach slowing walking back to the dugout, an obvious move that let the reliever throw a few more pitches while getting warm in a hurry.

Gibbons threw a fastball that sailed way above Jorge's head for ball four. As Jorge walked to first, and the other two advancing, the bases were loaded for Billy. With one swing, he could make it a one-run game. However, it would not be against Gibbons as the Manager walked to the mound, slower than the pitching coach had left. Once he arrived at the mound, he waved his left hand in the air, indicating he wanted George Dewitt, the league leader among relievers. It was an apparent move to get a left-handed pitcher against the left-handed hitter Billy Tankersly.

Billy watched him warming up. He remembered something he had learned at Lexington, "if the reliever throws all of one kind of a pitch in his warmups, you can expect another type of a pitch on the first pitch to you."

He watched the reliever throw seven pitches in his warm up, and all were fastballs. Billy expected a curve away from him, but still on the corner of the plate because Dewitt could not afford to walk a batter.

The pitch was precisely as Billy thought - a curve on the outside of the plate. He was ready for it, slashing a ground ball to the third base side. He'd hoped to pull a ball on the right side to at least score one runner, but he felt he'd hit the ball hard enough to get it through the infield. The Reno third baseman backhanded the ball, planted his feet and rifled a strike to the Reno catcher for a force out at the plate, who then fired the ball to first to try to get Billy for a double play.

Billy thought he beat the throw, but the umpire did not care what Billy thought. He saw the ball touch the first baseman glove before Billy's toes came down on the bag.

In a sweeping motion, more than just raising his hand, the ump yelled out, "You're out."

Billy had hit into a double play leaving the score 5-0 in favor of Reno. However, Arturo and Jorge were now on second and third, and Omaha still had a chance to cut the Reno lead. Mack was up.

He had been hot the last month raising his batting average to .301, second on the team to Billy. Everyone in the Omaha dugout was cheering Mack on, watching him take three straight pitches, all balls. Obviously, Dewitt did not want to let Mack hit and walked him on the next pitch.

The bases were loaded again as Enrique strode to the batter's box. He had won two games during the year with bases loaded hits, so he had confidence as he adjusted his gloves, peering at DeWitt. The first pitch was a strike on the inside corner. Enrique did not even turn or say anything; he knew it had hit the corner of the plate.

He was expecting a fastball on the second pitch and was fooled with a slider breaking away. Enrique knew it was a strike even before the ump raised his right hand. Two strikes, no balls. Enrique was in a hole but determined to drive in at least two runs.

It was not going to happen as Dewit threw a changeup that registered 74 on the radar gun. Enrique swung far ahead of the ball even reaching the plate. With the bases loaded twice in the same inning, Omaha could not score.

The rest of the game was pretty much the same. Omaha would threaten to score, but each time left runners on base. The final score was 5-0, and Billy had gone 0-4, only the second time since being promoted to Omaha.

25

A Dream Comes True

Coach Keller called a meeting in the clubhouse and immediately told the team all they had done wrong in this first game of the Triple A Championship. He addressed Billy's slashing a ball down the third-base line when his job was to hit the ball to the right side of the infield.

"Billy, you should have taken that first strike instead of trying to be a hero by hitting a ball down the line. The third baseman was playing very close to the line to prevent exactly what you did, and he outfoxed you," said the coach. "You should have taken an overview of the defense before you ever stepped into the box," Coach Keller concluded.

As the players filed out, the Coach called Billy into his office. Billy did not know what to expect.

"Billy, this was a lousy way to end your time this year with the Storm Chasers. However, Anderson is out for the year, and you are being called up to the Royals, effective immediately," Billy's coach smiled, as he gave Billy the words he'd visualized in his mind many times. "You are being called up to the Royals."

He really did not know what to expect as he packed his bags. He would make reservations on the first flight to KC. It was a short flight as Omaha was only 188 miles from Kansas City. He was returning home, but in a far different way than when he originally left two years ago.

He arrived at Kansas City's Municipal Airport and was greeted by Tom Hankins, the infield coach for the Royals.

"Billy, are we glad to see you," the coach started. "Skip is out for the year, and Pete Strong has been filling in at SS, but he's our utility second and third baseman, but does not have the speed to play SS. We've got one week left in our regular season, and we are one game out of reaching a playoff spot," the coach continued as the car drove toward Kauffman Stadium, where the Royals were going to play Detroit in the first of a three-game series at home.

"We are going to throw you into the starting lineup tonight, Billy," said the coach. He continued. "It's not an ideal situation for you, we understand. But, we've been following your minor league career, and everyone in the front office believes you have the right temperament to jump in and help the Royals reach the playoff spot."

Billy would be staying at the Hyatt Hotel on the Country Club Plaza. He checked in, admiring the beauty of the hotel, but his mind was on the game tonight. He'd be starting for the Kansas City Royals, a dream he had visualized many times. He had pictures of the players on his wall in Lexington and then Omaha.

The Royals were to be on the field taking batting practice 45 minutes after Billy arrived. After checking into the hotel, and depositing his belongings in his room, Coach Hankins waited in the lobby. Billy joined him, and they were on their way to Kauffman Stadium.

"Billy, you will be hitting ninth in the lineup tonight," Coach Hankins told Billy on the ride to the Stadium.

"Coach, do you know who is pitching for Detroit?" Billy asked.

"You will be facing Al Murphy, the ace for Detroit. We need to get to him fast as he gets better as the game wears on," Coach Hankins told Billy. "Since you will be hitting ninth, you probably can expect to see pitches you've never seen in the minors, Billy," the coach explained to Billy.

Billy had taken the drive many times into the parking lot between Kauffman Stadium and Arrowhead Stadium where the Kansas City Chief played. Always before, it was to watch a game, but tonight, he was going to be playing for the KC Royals. He wondered if the news came out so his Dad and Mom and Mr. Booker would be at the game. He had not had time to call them. Billy finally bought a cell phone, so he had no excuse for not calling them.

"Dad, do you and Mom know I've been promoted to the Royals and might even get into the game tonight?," Billy excitedly said to his Dad. "Obviously, we know and will be at the game," laughed Mr. Tankersly. Then Billy walked into the clubhouse that he hoped would be his "home" for many years to come.

"Billy," the Royals Manager, Ned Hall, started once he entered the clubhouse. "We know you are only 17 years old, and this is a major jump for you. Only a few other players have reached the major leagues at a younger age. Joe Nuxhall was the youngest at 15 years and 316 days. He was a starting pitcher who was thrown into the majors sort of like you. Joe went on to have a 22-year career in the majors and earned the title of Ol' Lefthander. So, Billy, hopefully, this is a start to a 22-year career for you," Coach Hall ended.

Billy dressed in his number 14 KC Royals uniform. He had never worn number 14 before but thought it was really fantastic to have Pete Rose's number. He walked down the clubhouse ramp to the diamond and looked over the crowd to see if his Dad or Mom or Mr. Booker would be in the stands. Not many fans were there yet, as Tommy Vargas told him it was his time in the cage to hit.

Billy remembered at Lexington being told the Royals played contact baseball, so he did not let many pitches go by without swinging. He hit a couple of nice line drives to left and put one over the right-field fence as his time in the cage ended.

He met many of the other players, even before getting in the cage, but almost the entire team was watching him like a hawk while he was hitting. Was he going to help the Royals with his hitting? After his time in the cage, several of the players talked about how maybe Billy Tankersly could help them reach the playoff spot.

All the players seemed to go back in the club-house after their swings in the cage and Billy did the same. He met Drakula, the famous reliever who no one wanted to hit against. His real name was Ralph Graff, and he was a closer who was regarded as one of the best, if not the best reliever in the game today.

He met each of the position players, Mike Thomas, the third baseman who had already hit a career-high 34 HRs; and the second basemen, Jerry Fairfield, who had played at Lexington and Omaha the past two years. Like Billy, he was still considered a rookie since he'd only played half the season with the Royals. Then he met the first baseman, Harvey Hos, who was known for his hitting and fielding. He had won something like three or four straight gold gloves given to the best defensive player of that position. This year so far, he had hit his career number of HR's as well as Thomas at 3B.

The more players Billy met, the more he felt like pinching himself. "Was he really on the same team as these guys?" he thought to himself, knowing they had won the World Series two years ago.

Before he knew it, he heard the ump yell "play ball!" as Wes Oliver took the mound for the Royals. He had a respectable 3.76 ERA, but he was not as consistent as the team hoped for. This was an important game as they could tie Oakland for the playoff spot, either if Oakland lost or remain one game behind if the Royals won and Oakland won its game tonight. The Royals would naturally be watching the big scoreboard in center field to see how the Oakland-Minnesota game was going.

Billy heard his name over the PA system. "Billy Tankersly at SS, batting eighth."

He had not even looked at the lineup before the game. Ned, the manager, told him he'd be starting and hitting ninth, he thought. But eighth or ninth, he was confident enough to believe that he'd be hitting much higher in the lineup after a few games because he intended to show them that he was their new shortstop for not only this year but for years to come.

26

Billy's First Major League Game

Standing on the field, looking up at the full house of Kansas City fans, should have made Billy nervous, but more than anything, he was looking for his Dad and Mom and Mr. Booker. He wondered if there had even been time for a story in the Kansas City Star about his promotion.

The first batter for the Tigers was Prescott Phillips, the Tigers SS who was a speedster and had stolen 15 bases this year and only been caught five times.

He took Oliver's first pitch. It was called a strike. Billy looked around the stadium, checking where the shadows were for this 7:05 PM start. Billy had attended enough games at Kauffman know where the shadows were, but he still was studying everything he could when Phillips hit a ball to his right. He backhanded it quickly and fired to Hos to record the first out.

The next two hitters struck out against Oliver, so it appeared this was going to be one of his good games.

The second baseman, Jerry Fairfield, led off for the Royals. He took the count to 3-2 before swinging at a curveball that bounced off the plate.

Hos was standing next to Billy, putting his arm around him, he told Billy, "Up here, Billy, the pitching is going to be much better than anyone you saw, even at Omaha. That ball that bounced on the plate was the type of pitch you will see up here. It looks good when it leaves the pitcher's hand, but drops from the beltline to hitting the plate like the pitch to Jerry. My advice would be to take as many pitches as necessary to get a feel for the pitcher," Hos concluded.

While Hos was talking to Billy, Harmon Kane, the centerfielder came up and slashed a double down the third base line.

Batting third for the Royals was Mike Thomas with Hos hitting cleanup. Thomas was a right-handed hitter. He took a couple of pitches, both for strikes. The Tigers played for Mike to pull the ball and had their SS in short left field. Billy wondered why Mike did not hit to right field. Then he saw why.

Thomas hit the ball into the fountains in center-field. The noise in Kauffman was deafening. Mike jogged around the bases at a pretty good pace consid-ering he had just hit one of the longest balls Billy had ever seen. He and Hos did a chest bump as Mike scored. The Royals led, 2-0 with only one out as Hos stepped into the batter's box.

On the first pitch, Hos drilled one that went over the right-field fence, for back-to-back home runs. The players in the dugout decided to act like Hos had not done anything. They ignored him as he returned to the dugout. No one said, "nice hit" or anything. They just were quiet. No one on the team said anything to Hos and Billy had no idea what was going on. Why weren't they chest bumping Hos and yelling nice hit? Then he realized. It was a joke on Hos. Before Billy had time to figure it all out, the players were patting Hos on the head or butt, and telling him "Way to go, Hos." Billy's mind was on what was happening in the dugout, almost as a spectator. Then his mind came back to reality, realizing soon he was going to have his first at bat in the major leagues.

The next batter, Al Bourno, the right fielder, got good wood on the second pitch, but it was a line drive right at the 3B for Detroit.

Batting sixth was Juan Perez, the catcher. He hit a ball so hard it bounced out of the gate in left field, rolling to the parking lot. Unfortunately, it was foul. He struck out on the next pitch.

The Tigers did not score in the top of the second, and Billy was going to be the second man up this inning. As he stood in the on deck circle, swinging a heavy bat, studying the pitcher, he could not help but look up in the grandstands for his Dad and Mom and Mr. Booker. All of a sudden, he saw his Mom waving to him frantically. Then he saw his Dad and Mr. Booker. Billy had no idea if it was proper to wave or not, but he did anyway. He was thrilled that they would see his first major league game.

Nick Gordon, the left fielder, batted before Billy, and he hit a pop up to the second baseman of the Tigers. It was now Billy's turn to bat. He felt nervous and yet excited. He knew he was going to get a hit. At least, he visualized it.

"Strike one," said the umpire in a low voice. He added, "Inside corner." He did not know if that was for Billy's benefit or not, but he was grateful for the extra information.

On the second pitch, Billy hit a curveball on the outside corner of the plate to left field. It was a hard line drive, and even though he rounded first ready to head to second, he saw the left fielder already throwing to second. Billy had just hit a line drive single in his first at-bat in the Major Leagues. How could life be any better? He looked up into the grandstands to see his folks and Mr. Booker jumping up and down. It was a moment he would never forget.

Billy had gone over the signals with the coaches before the game, and he was sure he remembered all of them. Naturally, he looked for the steal sign, not really expecting it in his first major league game. However, he saw the third base coach, Coach Bodine, slid his hand across his chest after several other movements. Billy was sure that was the steal sign, but he was so excited that he was not sure. He questioned himself, "what should I do...I think it's the steal sign."

He took his lead off first, not quite as big as he had been taking at Omaha because he had not seen Murphy pitch. "Back!" shouted the first base coach. Billy was already diving for the bag. He knew he was safe but now knew a little more about Murphy's pickoff move.

Billy took a slightly bigger lead and was diving back to first again as Murphy used a different pickoff move. Everyone knew Billy has safe, but Billy was happy to have seen Murphy's second pickoff move.

On the first pitch to Curtis Alverez, the DH hitter, Billy was off. He did not look back and dove head first to second base, grabbing the corner of the bag as he went past it with his speed. He really did not hear the umpire but saw his hands outstretched meaning Billy had his first stolen base in the major leagues.

"I'm on my way to breaking Ricky Henderson record," Billy thought to himself. He looked in, trying to get the signals of the next pitch to let Curtis know what was coming, but the catcher flashed at least ten signs, and Billy had no idea what pitch the pitcher was throwing on the next pitch, but was on his toes for a wild pitch or passed ball.

The pitch bounced a foot in front of the plate, and Curtis laid off it, but the Detroit catcher was not able to hold on to it as it bounced about five feet to the right. Billy was off. The throw was hurried, and Billy had his second stolen base.

"Good job, Billy," said Coach Bodine. "It would have taken a perfect throw to get you, with your speed," the coach added.

It felt strange to Billy. "This was no different than Lexington or Omaha," he thought. "It's still baseball."

Curtis hit a sacrifice fly ball to centerfield, and Billy scored easily to make it 3-0 in favor of the Royals.

The game ended with that same score. Billy had no more hits in his two additional times up to the plate. He struck out once and hit a long fly ball to deep left field that he thought might get out of the park, but the wind held it up, and it was just a long fly ball out. He handled four ground balls and one popup with no problem. Several Royals congratulated him on a good game. Coach Bodine was the most vocal, and he praised Billy in front of the team.

"Hey guys," he said in the clubhouse. "You guys played great today and made some outstanding plays to keep Al out of trouble. Billy, you made a great play in the fifth inning when you backhanded what was a sure hit, threw the guy out, and even beat him by a full step. Great play in your first major league game," the coach concluded. The other Royals started chanting, "way to go, Billy Tankersly, way to go Billy."

He was embarrassed but enjoyed the Kansas City Royals players commenting on his first game. Billy was in seventh heaven.

However, seeing his parents and Mr. Booker made it like eighth heaven. They ate dinner at Joe's Barbeque. When Billy left Kansas City, it was known as Oklahoma Joe's, and he never could understand how an Oklahoma BBQ place could be the best BBQ restaurant in KC. After all, Kansas City was known as the BBQ capital of the world. Now that it was Joe's, he figured while he was away, some of the locals insisted they change the name to just Joe's.

"Son, we are all so proud of you," said his Dad over dinner. "We all are," Mr. Booker chimed in. "You played a great game, but to think you've made the Royals in two short years since you turned pro is pretty fantastic.

"Son," Billy's Dad started. Billy always knew it was something serious when his Dad started a conversation that way. "Mom has been extremely successful in her business, and I'm considering quitting my job and joining her," his Dad finished.

That news made Billy respect his parents even more if that was possible. He thought, "what great teammates."

Mr. Booker was the one who ended dinner saying, "I'm getting too old to stay out late, so hate to do so, but I have to leave and put my body in bed."

Billy's folks agreed although they were doing it so Billy could get a good night's sleep. They offered him a ride to the hotel, and he rode with them in the back seat like nothing had changed since he was a young boy...except, he was now playing for the Kansas City Royals, his lifelong dream.

<u>27</u>

Playoff Game

Billy provided new life to the Royals, and they went on to win three of their next four games, and all but cinched getting to the playoffs. There was one more game, and they won it.

Billy was getting to play in a playoff game, his first year in the majors.

They would be playing the Houston Astros in a one-game playoff to see who would be facing the American League East team in the best of five game series. The game was in Houston as they also had a better record than the Royals did.

The team gathered at the stadium and rode the bus to their chartered flight to Houston. Hos sat next to Billy on the flight down, and they talked about Hos's days at Omaha.

"I remember playing for Coach Keller at Omaha," Hos began. "I'm not sure you realize it, but Mike, Al, Juan, and Figgie, our starting pitcher in tomorrow's game, and I all played at Omaha together before reaching the majors."

Billy responded with a statement that floored Hos.

"Hos, I lived in KC and followed all of you when you were playing for Omaha. My only dream was to play for the Royals, but never in my wildest dreams would I have thought I'd be playing for the Royals in my second year of pro ball," Billy added.

"None of us made it that fast, Billy, but it's obvious to me after seeing you play in the last five or six games that you are a real talent," Hos said, in a way that made it seem like he was a little envious of Billy. However, it also made Billy realize even more that he was good enough to be playing with these major leaguers.

"Hos, I appreciated your compliment, but my goal is to break Ricky Henderson's stolen base record," Billy started. "Do you know how many bases he stole, Hos?" Billy asked.

"1406, Billy," Hos smiled. "You'll find out up here that we are all shooting for a record of some kind, and we know stats like no one you've ever been around."

"Let me give you an example," Hos continued. "All of us know your stats at Lexington and Omaha."

"No way," Billy's voice was a little higher than normal. "Are you kidding me?" Billy asked.

"You had 27 stolen bases before you were promoted to Omaha and 17 while playing for the Storm Chasers," Hos said, matter of factly.

"Wow, I'm amazed," replied Billy.

"Something else we know about you. Your weak spot is inside, down low," Hos laughed.

Billy was amazed. He did not even know what to say except smile back at Hos, saying "yes sir."

The next day, the team took batting and infield practice just to stay loose for tomorrow's game.

After the light workout, Billy decided to call Bobby, who he had not talked to in ages. In fact, he did not think he had talked to his best friend since he was promoted to the Royals.

"Hey Bobby, how you doing?" Billy asked.

"Well, not as good as you," Bobby replied. "Congratulations on making it to the Royals and starting no less. I know you made it faster than most, Billy, just because you visualized it and worked so hard. I'm proud of you, best friend."

"Thanks, Bobby. I really appreciate that. Now, how fast are you going to make it up here in the big time?" Billy responded.

"I'm not far behind, Billy. I ended up hitting 36 HRs at Lexington. Never did get promoted to Omaha, but am hoping after Spring Training next year, I'll be playing for the Storm Chasers and who knows, maybe someone will get hurt and I'll join you next year," Bobby laughed.

"Hey Bobby, did you ever asked Emma out?" Billy quizzed his best buddy.

"Well... I wanted to talk to you about that, Billy," Bobby replied. "I know you really like her, so I've hesitated in even asking her out."

"Wow, that is really nice of you, Bobby. Thank you," Billy said, understanding that only a best friend would do something like that.

"I hereby release you from anything keeping you from asking her out, if you want to," said Billy, wondering if he was doing the right thing as Emma had been the only girl on his mind all season.

"I'd love to, Billy. Are you sure it's ok with you?" Bobby asked.

"No," Billy laughed, "but ask her out anyway."

The young men talked about the game tomorrow when Billy realized he needed to be in bed.

"I've got to go, Bobby; we have a game tomorrow," Billy laughed.

Billy took his bat to bed with him and wondered if a wife would ever understand him sleeping with his bat. He laughed at that thought. He slept soundly, and before he knew it, the players were on the bus for the Houston ballpark.

The fans were loud, pulling for their Astros to win this one game playoff. Billy was hitting seventh, but wishing Royals management would realize his speed and bat him leadoff, his favorite spot in the batting order.

The innings went by fast. The Royals were trailing 6-2 going into the eighth inning. Billy had made two good plays at SS but had not gotten a hit or on base his first two times up. He knew he would be batting this inning. The season had come down to one game for the Royals and one game for the Astros. Both managers were using their relievers, and even their starters would probably get in, in this game. There would be no more games to be played this season if the Royals lost.

As Billy strode to the batter's box, Tracy Muggins, the manager for the Astros, walked to the mound to bring in his left-handed starter, Conrade Jennings, to face the left-handed hitting Billy Tankersly. Two men were on base as Jennings finally finished his warmups. Billy was visualizing hitting one over the short right field fence as he stepped into the batter's box.

The crowd was so loud; he could not hear the umpire yelling out strikes or balls. He had never been in a game like this.

Billy took the first two pitches, a ball, and a strike. On the third pitch, he saw the ball all the way to his bat. It was the pitch Billy had been hoping to see the first two times up. This would be the last time Billy would see a fastball inside because he hit it into the seventh or eighth row in the right-field seats. The crowd went silent as Billy rounded the bases to be met at the plate by Mike, Hos, and most of the team. The score was now 6-5 with the Royals having new life.

Nick Gordon followed Billy's HR with a double into the left-field corner. With the tying run on second base, Muggins walked to the mound to change pitchers again. Both Managers were using everyone on the team to win this game. There would be no more games, for the losing team.

This time, Muggins brought in their closer to stop the Royals from tying the game. But it was too late as Juan, who had been in a slump and dropped down to the number eight slot in the batting order, singled on the first pitch, scoring Gordon from second and the game was tied.

The top of the eighth ended with the game being tied, going into the bottom of the eighth inning, with Houston's middle of the order coming up. Ned Hall, the Royals manager, was taking no chances, as he brought in the Royals closer, Ralph Graff, otherwise known as "Drakula."

It only took one pitch to put the Astros back in the lead again. Bill Monroe hit it over the short left field wall, and the crowd was even louder than it had been. Drakula struck the next three batters out, but going into the top of the ninth, the Royals were on the verge of playing their last game of the season.

It was the top of the batting order for the Royals. Fairfield, Kane, and Thomas were the first three hitters with Hos fourth up if one of the others got on base.

Fairfield hit a slug bunt down the third base line. The Astros third baseman had been guarding the baseline to prevent a double down the line. He rushed in, picked the ball up barehanded and fired to first, but he was not even close to getting Jerry out. The Royals had a chance with the tying run on first. Billy thought, "What will Coach Hall signal to Kane? A sacrifice bunt to get the tying run in scoring position?" He was somewhat surprised that Coach Bodine, acting on a signal from the Manager on the bench, signaled for Kane to hit away.

Billy thought, "That's taking a chance on a double play, why not bunt?" Before he had his thought out, Harmon hit one that bounced off the left-field wall and halfway back to the infield. He ended up at 2B with Jerry reaching 3B. Now, with two runners in scoring position, Mike Thomas came up, hoping to drive in the lead run. He was not looking for a pitch to drive into the right-field stands. Billy thought, "He is a professional and a major leaguer so he will not be swinging for the fences like Billy had in his first Little League game."

Once again, Tracy Muggins, the Astros' manager ambled to the mound. You could tell his mind was going a mile a minute, but everyone knew what he was going to do. He waved his right hand to bring in Scooter Jones, who was also a starter for the Astros. Muggins was doing everything in his power to get the Astros into the real playoffs, but it made no difference to the Royals player Mike Thomas. He drilled a line drive down the right field line, scoring both of the runners and ended up at second base. The Royals had the lead, 7-6. Jones did not give up another hit, so going into the bottom of the ninth, the Royals had a one-run lead that they had to protect.

Billy wondered who Coach Hall was going to bring in to pitch and was surprised to see Drakula back on the mound. All the Royals had to do was protect their one-run lead.

Drakula took the count to 3-2 before striking out the leadoff hitter for the Astros.

"Only two more outs and we've won the division," thought Billy standing at SS.

The next batter hit a sharp grounder over 2B. Jerry could not reach it, but Billy was close. He picked the ball up, twirled around, almost 360 degrees, and threw a strike to Hos.

He watched the umpire indicating "safe." Coach Hall came out to argue that the runner was out by a mile. He asked to get the opinion of another umpire, but finally, the coach asked for a replay in the NY office. He was only allowed one replay request per game unless he won that protest. If he won the protest, the Royals would be allowed another protest.

The umpires huddled together by the batter's box of the Astros. It seemed like forever, but Billy watched the umpires taking their headsets off, and the chief umpire signaled "safe." The crowd noise was almost unbearable. Not only had the Royals used their only protest, but also the Astros had the tying run on first base.

Coach Hall immediately went to the mound to talk to Drakula. He decided to let him pitch to one more batter.

Billy was in the thick of a major league playoff game and knew that the Royals had to keep the man on first from scoring. Billy was ready if a ball was hit to him. He looked over to Jerry, indicating Jerry should take any steal attempt, but neither player expected the Astros' runner to try to steal off Drakula.

Billy could see the signs Jose was giving Drakula. The first was a curve, hopefully hitting the inside corner. It was a ball. The next pitch was a fastball low, so the count was 2-0, and no way could Drukula put the winning run on base. The next pitch was almost over Juan's head, but thankfully, he caught it so the runner could not advance, but it was a 3-0 count. Ralph, alas Drakula, could not afford to throw another ball. He had to get the ball over the plate.

Drakula hit the center of the plate, and Tommy Jennings, the right fielder for the Astros, swung on the 3-0 count with a mighty swing. He made contact. Billy could tell from the crack of the bat even over the cheering fans. He knew Jennings had hit it solid. He watched as the ball hit the base of the right-field fence. Al picked it up and threw a strike to Hos, who relayed the ball to Juan as the runner was about to score. It was too late, the Astros had tied the game in the bottom of the ninth, and now the Royals had to keep Jennings from scoring.

Coach Hall walked to the mound, signaling for Butch Kelly to come in. Kelly was a right-handed pitcher that barely threw 88 mph, but had a wicked curveball.

He struck out the left fielder for the Astros, so now it was up to George Conner the DH for the Astros who had hit 26 HRs during the regular season.

Kelly threw a curve that broke late, and Conner missed it by a lot. That gave Billy more hope as he was thinking, "If Butch can get Conner out, I'll get to bat in the top of the tenth."

Two more pitches and Kelly recorded another strikeout. The game was now going into extra innings. Billy could not remember a game like this in all the games he had played.

Billy was second up. Nick Gordon was leading off the inning. He hit a one-shot bouncer to the SS who threw Nick out with ease. It was now Billy's turn.

He had been watching the Astros' pitcher during his warmups and when he was pitching to Nick. He saw on the scoreboard that his second pitch to Nick hit 100 mph. Billy had never faced a pitcher who threw that fast except for the Royals pitcher who came out to the Leawood Training Center one day and threw a 99 mph pitch at Billy. It was fast, but he hit it, so he knew he could hit the Astros pitcher, and on the second pitch, he did exactly that by hitting a hard line drive over the second baseman's head. He had to hold at first base but was hoping to get the steal sign.

Billy wondered if he would get a steal sign in this situation. He did not have to wonder a long time as Coach Bodine hit his hat with his left hand, which was the steal signal for this game.

The young speedster took off the minute the pitcher's foot crossed the mound. He did not think he had ever run this fast. He saw the second baseman getting ready to catch the ball. Billy knew it was going to be close. He dove for second base like he had so many other times.

He caught the corner of the bag with his left hand and knew without a doubt that he'd beaten the throw. The umpire agreed with him as his arms swung out to indicate Billy was safe. He could not hear the umpire over the crowd, but saw the safe sign, and took the biggest breath of air he'd ever taken. He heard himself say, "Thank you, God." It was probably the most critical steal Billy had made in all his years of baseball.

Juan did not waste a swing. He hit the first pitch in the gap between left and center field. Billy scored easily, even though Juan stayed at first base. The Royals led once again, 8-7.

The next two batters for the Royals struck out. Going into the bottom of the tenth, the Royals had a one-run lead, just as they had in the ninth inning.

Coach Kelly made the decision to leave Butch in. He had not given up a home run all year. It was not surprising because as slow as Butch pitched, the batter had to almost be Superman to hit one even to the wall.

Billy watched the first Astros hitter fan on a 0-2 count. Billy Tankersly was now two outs away from winning the most crucial game in his young life.

The second Astros hitter swung and missed a 65 mph curve, topping the ball in front of the plate. Juan jumped on it and threw the runner out. Now with two outs, the Royals were one out away from playing Baltimore in the American League championship game.

"The next hitter is hopefully the last," Billy thought as he watched Butch going into his windup. The ball was hit softly toward Billy. He ran in, picked the ball up barehanded and fired to Hos at first. The umpire signaled safe. Billy wanted to argue, but he knew it wouldn't do any good.

With a man on first, Billy signaled to Jerry that he would take a throw from Juan if they tried to steal. Two outs, so all the team needed was to get one more out. The batter for the Astros was their home run leader, "Sweet Spot" Cohen, but Butch Kelly had not given up a home run all year, so Billy was not worried about Cohen hitting one out of the park.

He was wrong. Cohen hit Kelly's slow pitch over the short left field fence, and the Astros had won the playoff game and the opportunity to play Baltimore. The Royals were going home, one out from having a chance to play in the World Series.

No words were spoken in the clubhouse. Everyone was quiet. What was there to say?

28

Being Home

The flight back to KC was just as quiet. Everyone was thinking, "One more out." There were no words to express the disappointment of the team, who had worked for this day, thinking they could beat the Astros. With Billy being a rookie who might not even make the team next year when Skip Anderson was healed, his thoughts were more on next year than on the loss the team had just experienced.

The plane set down at KC's International Airport, and the team was pleased to see several thousand fans waving their Royal blue hats and whatever else they had to wave. There were a few attempted smiles, and a few autographs signed, but their season was over after starting the season with one goal, to win the pennant.

Billy walked through the terminal, mostly unnoticed as the stars of the Royals were hounded for autographs. Hos was signing a hat for a fan when Billy saw his Dad. He went running toward him, jumping up and hugging him before even seeing his Mom or Mr. Booker. They all hugged Billy, and he heard his Dad say, "Let's get out of here and get something to eat."

Billy got his luggage and his bat that he used in his last at-bat in the playoff game. He knew that would be his sleeping partner for an entire winter.

They ate at Winstead's, as Billy said all he wanted was a hamburger from Winsteads, his childhood hangout. Everyone was praising Billy for reaching the Royals in only his second year, but all he could think about was, "Will I be able to stay on the Royals roster after Spring Training?"

He was staying at his folk's house, and his Dad stayed up talking to Billy about his season, with the Legends, the Storm Chasers and finally the Royals. They sat out on the front porch and Billy told his Dad about each stop, some of the players he expected to reach the majors in a year or two, and what he thought his chances were of making the Royals next year.

"Dad, I really want to thank you for all the help you have been, and I really want nothing more than to make you proud," Billy told his Dad.

"What about Ricky Henderson's record?" his Dad asked.

For the first time since the game was over, Billy smiled, "Oh yeah, that." His Dad laughed with him.

He told his Dad and Mom "good night" and headed toward his room to call Bobby. They both had graduated from Skyping and were using the Face-Time feature on their iPhones.

"Hey Bobby," he began. "Guess you know all the news I've got, what about you?"

"That was really a tough break, Billy. Only one more out and you guys would be playing Baltimore right now," spoke Bobby in a tone not usual for their conversations. "When you hit that home run, I really thought the Royals were going to make a comeback and win the game."

"Yeah Bobby, me too, no pennant this year, but I'm three stolen bases closer to Ricky's record," Billy laughed, trying to get the conversation on a positive note.

"So what about you?" Billy asked.

Bobby was more than eager to tell Billy about his first year in the pros. "I hit 25 home runs in only half a season."

"Wow, Bobby, you've really developed power," Billy said, with his mind completely off the Royals loss. "Will you be coming to Spring Training in Surprise, Arizona next year?

"Billy, ever since I was drafted by the Royals, even though I wasn't a first-round pick like you, I know inside I can and will be playing on the Royals. Yes, I have been invited to Surprise next year."

"Wow, that is great news, Bobby," Billy excitedly exclaimed. He might have been more excited about that news than his own promotion to the Royals. Billy had missed his best friend, and just to think that they might be playing together one day again, made him forget about the loss.

"Bobby, let's go early to camp, and I can show you around and give you an idea of what to expect," Billy said, already thinking about spring training, only one day after losing the biggest game of his career.

"I'm just excited that we get to be together on a field again, Billy," said his best friend.

"Well, spring training doesn't work that way exactly," Billy, laughed. "We probably won't be on a field together in the beginning, only if I get demoted to Omaha again, and you get promoted to Omaha will we be able to play together. My hunch is that Skip Anderson will be back to the Royals next year, and I'll probably end up at Triple A," Billy continued.

"Well, I intend to show off my power in Spring Training to make sure the Royals management sees how valuable I can be to the organization," Bobby said, matter-of-factly.

Billy laughed. "That was my attitude last spring, Bobby. I was determined to make Royals management see me, and know what I could do to help the Royals," he said.

"Hey, I have a question for you, Bobby, you played with Bill Ostoff a lot of the year, right?" Billy asked.

"Yes, Bill and I became good friends. Why do did you ask?" Bobby quizzed his friend.

"I always called him Billy O, but he was a guy on the Legends that I liked, but never really got to know," Billy explained. "I just imagined him as someone who would make the Royals and have the chance to really become a star."

"Yeah, he'll be at Spring Training," Bobby said. "I agree with you, Billy Ostoff is definitely someone who will be playing for the Storm Chasers next year, and who knows, maybe the Royals, if he gets a break like you got."

"You can say that again. Had Skip not been injured, I may not have ever made the Royals. They might have traded me first," Billy explained about his own feelings about making the Royals this year.

"You were a number one draft pick, Billy. They were not going to trade you. In fact, I read that you signed for $2.4 million, is that right?" Bobby asked.

"Yes, I guess nothing is private in today's world," Billy moaned, realizing everyone knew how much he was making. "Bobby, that sounds like a lot of money, but unless you make the bigs, the money we get paid in the minors is peanuts, so that signing bonus is supposed to last me five years if I did not make the Royals," Billy informed his best bud.

"Yeah, but you got promoted to the 40-man roster, which means you are making some good money right now, in addition to $2.4 million," Bobby laughed.

"For those players on the 40-man roster for the first time, who get sent back to the minors, there is a minimum of about $40,000 a month. Obviously, that is extremely high compared to the average person working for a living or a minor leaguer, but we have to pay for our own lodging, meals, etc. They also give us a living allowance that is about $100 a day, so I'm definitely not complaining" Billy started.

"Bobby, I don't know what you signed for, but I read an article before even getting drafted that said something like, 'a minor leaguer not on a 40-man roster gets paid at archaic rates that are comically low'. Does that describe you so far, Bobby, because it sure applied to me until being put on the 40-man roster?" Billy enjoyed laughing with his friend.

Bobby interrupted his friend as he always does, "Billy, my signing bonus was for a little over $500,000, but my starting salary was only $1100 a month. That was only for a maximum of five months during the season. So, if I had stayed in the Rookie league, I would have only made $6,000 for the entire year. I read where most minor leaguers make less than the poverty level, so the signing bonus is critical, and even being promoted to Double A, I can tell you I am still below the poverty line." Bobby ended his explanation with information that Billy already knew because he was paid the same, until his promotion to the Royals.

"Well, my goal next year will be to make the 40-man roster like you did, Billy," said Bobby, again matter of factly.

"I hope you do, but it was a very lucky break for me this year. With Skip back, I hate to admit it, but I'll probably be back at Omaha," Billy moaned.

"Hey, where is my optimistic friend, who always sees the bright side?" Bobby asked.

"OK, Bobby, you are right. I'm going to beat out Skip Anderson for the starting SS position for the Royals next year.....and I'm going to steal 60 bases," Billy said as was already visualizing.

<u>29</u>

Mr. Booker and Coach Heier

Billy didn't lose any time in starting his off season workouts. He called Mr. Booker and asked if he'd run with him that afternoon.

"Billy, to be honest, I'm not sure I can run anymore. Getting old isn't as great as it's cracked up to be," Mr. Booker said, being open and frank with his young student.

"Hey, you are the man who taught me to keep running every waking moment," Billy laughed, hoping to get his coach to at least try to run with him.

"Billy, maybe if I had my knees replaced, I could, but as it is, I'm having a hard time walking from one room to the next," Mr. Booker explained. "I do have an idea though. I'd bet Coach Heier would run with you, while I just sit back and give directions."

"Let's go over to the Academy and see if Coach Heier is there," Mr. Booker offered.

"Sounds good. Can you walk at all?" Billy asked.

"I'll pick you up in 15 minutes. I can still drive," he chuckled.

Billy was waiting outside, with his metal spikes hung over his shoulders. It reminded him of his first walk into the Lexington clubhouse. He was excited to see Mr. Booker come around the corner in a convertible.

"Holy smokes," Billy yelled. "You can't walk, so you go out and buy a convertible," Billy joked.

"Hey, it makes me feel younger, even if I do have a handicap sticker," Mr. Booker shot back, with a smile in his voice.

On the way to the Academy, Mr. Booker told Billy he'd watched the playoff game on TV and was really proud of Billy.

"It was great to see you hit that homer, Billy, and steal a base, but what I liked most watching was your defense. On that ball hit behind second base in the last or maybe next to the last inning, I'm not sure which, you showed off a lot more range than Anderson has ever had for the Royals," Mr. Booker continued.

"Really, Mr. Booker?" Billy asked, thinking to himself that he'd never compared his range against Anderson's.

"Skip has played more than 1000 games at SS for the Royals, and to anyone paying attention, his range has diminished quite a bit. His contract is through next year, so I imagine the Royals will keep him. Personally, I think you have a great chance to beat him out for the starting spot next year," Mr. Booker told Billy, encouraging him beyond anything Billy expected to get from today's practice session with his running coach.

"Gezzzz, Mr. Booker, you know how to encourage someone," Billy smiled.

"Billy, you need to see yourself as a major leaguer now. When you go to Spring Training, you should have one goal.....to beat out Anderson for the starting role in the opening game of the season," Mr. Booker continued.

They arrived at the Academy, and Coach Heier was at his desk as they approached him.

Coach Heier looked up to see Billy and Mr. Booker.

"Billy Tankersly, a major leaguer coming to see me," the coach said, definitely excited to see Billy again.

Billy went over to the coach and gave him a big hug, saying, "Coach Heier, you really helped me, in so many ways. You taught me, like Mr. Booker, to never doubt myself. You taught me to always, in every game I ever played, to walk away knowing I'd given my best, and that is exactly what I've done, Coach."

"I know that Billy, just watching you play in that playoff game. You know what I thought was the best play you made, not counting the homer and stolen base.....that dribbler to you in the last inning. Even though the runner was called safe, and I personally question that, you made a perfect throw after picking the ball up barehanded on the run, Coach Heier told the young man who was now much bigger and more filled out than he had been the last time the coach had seen Billy.

"I thought he was out too, coach," Billy agreed.

"Well, what are your goals for next year?" asked the man, who Billy admired more than anyone except maybe his Dad and Mr. Booker.

"My first goal is just to make the team next year instead of being sent back to Omaha," Billy answered.

"Billy, are you the same Billy Tankersly who grew up here at the Academy? You should be thinking about what your batting average is going to be at the end of next year, and how many bases you will have stolen, edging closer to Ricky's record," Coach Heier responded, almost before Billy had answered his question.

"Yes, sir. You are right. I've been so excited about this past year, I've sort of forgotten to always think big like you, and Mr. Booker taught me, but you taught me well. I imagine another day of listening to the words of the two of you again, and I'll have my head on properly and be thinking about next year," Billy replied, looking up to the two men who had made it possible for him to be the baseball player he was this year. He thought to himself, "I'm going to be bigger, stronger and a year older, so I should be thinking about beating out Anderson for the starting nod next year."

After visiting, Coach Heier told Billy to put on his spikes because he was going to be timed from the plate to first base. Billy was more than ready.

His first attempt was timed by Mr. Booker at 3.8 seconds.

"Billy, that was good, but you've had a full year to get better, and you hit 3.8 last year. Let's do it again with you hitting 3.7 this time," Mr. Booker pushed the almost 18 year old.

Billy ran to first, again and again until he was utterly exhausted and not even able to run. His best time had been 3.7 seconds, but he truly believed he could do better than that.

"Mr. Booker, will you come here tomorrow and push me until I can hit 3.5?" Billy asked.

"It may take until Spring Training to get you that low, but I do have a suggestion," Mr. Booker responded. I want you to mentally imagine that you have already hit that mark. When you go to sleep tonight, I want you thinking about hitting 3.5 in Spring Training. If you do that, the chances are good, you'll hit it and maybe exceed that mark before you go to camp. If you show that kind of speed, the Royals will have to keep you on the major league team, if nothing more than your ability to win a game with your speed," Mr. Booker continued pushing his young student, just like he had for the three years before Billy got signed.

"However, Billy," Mr. Booker added, "Jensen, the left fielder for the Royals hit 3.5 this year, so if you equal or beat that, you are going to turn heads."

The rest of the winter seemed to go by faster than most. It did not snow in Kansas City all winter for the first time in many years. Billy spent the time at the Academy, being coached by Mr. Booker, and Coach Heier. On days he didn't run, he would drive out to Kauffman Stadium, just to imagine himself leaving the stadium after a game. He would sit in the parking lot, just visualizing.

One weekend morning, he drove out to the stadium and was just sitting in the parking lot when a lot of cars started streaming in. Billy realized the Chiefs were playing that day at Arrowhead Stadium which sat next to Kauffman Stadium. He knew he'd better get out before the mass arrived because the Chiefs had the support of Kansas City fans the same as the Royals.

He drove home and decided to call Bobby. Billy wondered if Bobby was working as hard as he was this offseason. Spring Training was just weeks away, and Billy was more excited than ever, not just because he was returning as the starting SS, but because Bobby was going to be there. He also wondered if Bobby had ever asked Emma out.

"Hey Billy, what's up?" asked Bobby.

"I have a question for you, Bobby. Did you ever ask Emma out?" Billy asked.

Bobby started laughing. "No, I thought you were interested in Emma, so I wouldn't ask her out even if I wanted to do so."

"You are a great friend, Bobby. I sort of figure you would because you've always been more aggressive than me," stated Billy.

"What are you talking about Billy? I've never been as aggressive as you. I've always admired you for that."

"You are nuts," Billy laughed. "So you never asked her out?" Billy asked again.

"No Billy," said his Skype and now FaceTime mate for almost four years now. "So as soon as we're off here, give her a call. I know she would love to hear from you."

Billy debated, but instead of calling her, he called Mr. Booker.

"Are you watching the Chief's game?" Billy asked as Mr. Booker picked up the phone.

"Yes, I'm watching, but they have a big lead. What did you have in mind?" Mr. Booker asked.

"I'd like to go to the Academy with you and have you time me one last time before I leave town for Spring Training," Billy answered.

"Spring Training is another three weeks away, Billy. What do you mean, "one last time before you leave town?"

"Well, I might fly to Lexington to see the Williams, the family I stayed with while playing for the Legend," Billy responded.

That afternoon, Billy Tankersly hit 3.6, but told his coaches, he would hit 3.5 before the season was over.

30

Billy Goes Back To Lexington...For A Date

Billy called Emma that night and was surprised that she had followed him from the Storm Chasers to the Royals, and was definitely proud of him. It took about five minutes of talking before Billy got the courage to ask if she'd be free for a date next week.

"Emma, ever since leaving Lexington, I've thought of you and would really like to take you out on a real date this coming Wednesday night," Billy finally said.

"Billy, I would love that. I've thought of you a lot too. Your best friend, Bobby, wouldn't let me forget you. He talked about you all the time. One night, he told me that he'd never ask me out because you were interested. I responded to him that if you were so interested, why hadn't you even called me?" Emma opened up.

"Ahhh, lack of courage, I guess," answered Billy. "But I'm calling now, and would love to see you next week," Billy said, with a lot more confidence than he had before making the call. It was good to hear Emma's voice.

"I'd love to see you and actually go out on a date with you Billy Tankersly," Emma spoke into the phone in a way that made it impossible for him not to fly to Lexington.

"I'll see you next Wednesday," Billy ended the call, excited to think about Emma again, instead of reaching 3.5 down to first base.

Billy kissed his Mom goodbye and stopped by his Dad's office to tell him good-bye.

The plane was on schedule, and Billy arrived at the Lexington airport at 11:55 AM, which was only four miles from downtown, and five miles to the Williams home.

He checked into the Hyatt Place hotel a little before 1:00 PM after talking the front desk staff into an early check-in. He realized being aggressive paid off in adult life as well as in baseball. He wanted to call Emma immediately. He knew she had a job working with her Dad at his business, but hoped maybe she had taken the day off. He called her.

"Hey Billy, you got in safely," she answered the phone. The fact that she knew it was Billy calling meant that she had him on her cell phone, and it showed his name. That sort of encouraged him to say, "do we have to wait until tonight to have our date?"

"No way, Mr. Tankersly, get your butt over here," she laughed. Billy was excited, relieved, and nervous all at the same time.

"On my way, Emma," Billy replied as he put his shoes back on and turned on his Uber app.

He arrived, and Emma came running out of the Williams home, throwing her arms around Billy and kissing him on the cheek.

"You know, Emma when you didn't come into the hotel when Bobby came to see me play, I was really impressed and thankful for you," Billy told this beautiful girl sitting next to him.

"From that moment on, I wanted to ask you out, but just never got the courage," Billy confessed.

"Billy, Billy, Billy. I would have loved to have gone out with you while you were in Lexington," Emma replied to the young man who was as nervous in this moment as he was in his first championship game.

"Ahhh, sure wish I'd known that," Billy smiled. "Emma, you are the most beautiful girl I've ever met, and I just didn't have the confidence to ask you out then. Obviously, since I'm here now, I now have the confidence, even if you are the most beautiful girl in the world," Billy gushed with a big smile on his face.

"Not quite, Billy, but I did want you to ask me out, and I'm thrilled that you have come to Lexington to see me," Emma smiled back.

For the rest of the afternoon and evening, they ran together in the park, sat on Emma's front porch and talked and talked. Emma wanted to know his emotions when being called up to the majors, how exciting was it to be playing with guys like Hos and Mike?

Billy answered all of Emma's questions, and it got Billy pumped up for Spring Training. It was fun talking to someone other than Mr. Booker about his experiences and hope for the future.

He was beginning to like her more than he probably should, and he knew it.

"Emma, let me ask you a few questions now," Billy started.

"Why are you not taken by some guy here in Lexington, or by one of the ballplayers who stay or has stayed with you?" asked the 18 year old, but who was more mature than many guys older than him.

"I've dated, Billy, but no one really attracted me," Emma answered. "Did you want me to say I've been waiting for you, Billy Tankersly," she chided, hoping Billy would say yes.

"To be honest, yes, I would have loved to hear you say that. I've never been in love with any girl. I have been so focused on baseball there has never been time to date," Billy explained.

"Well Billy, I will tell you that I've been waiting, with little hope, that there would be a day like this, where I could tell you how much I like you. You are the only guy who stayed with us who I really wanted to spend time with," Emma opened up her heart.

"Wow, Emma. You are the only girl I've wanted to spend time with since turning pro," Billy put his arms around Emma, holding her for the first time.

He leaned over to kiss her, and she responded in broad daylight on her front porch.

"Oh Billy," she said breathlessly after finally pulling away from Billy's lips, "you may never get rid of me now."

"I hope not," Billy laughed, a happier laugh than he had ever felt. He felt warm and tingly inside. "Will you come to my games, wherever that might be?" Billy asked.

"Billy, I've got a job here in Lexington and can't really leave it, but might be able to get to some of your games," Emma replied.

The two of them talked and talked and spent as much time together as her work would allow. One day they went to a lake close to Lexington and Billy rented a boat, fishing equipment, and bait. The two of them sat in a boat for eight hours, catching crappie all day. Billy could not have done better if they'd hired a guide, but he wanted to be alone with Emma. Billy had only been fishing with his Dad once but had learned how to fix a fishing line, and getting the minnow's on the hook. He had no idea how to find a good place to fish but felt luck was with him as they caught a total of 16 fish, big enough to keep. Both had agreed on catching and releasing all their fish. But, he took pictures of Emma reeling in a nice size crappie.

When it got too dark to even see their lines, they took the boat back to where they had rented it, and the guy who rented it to them had left. There was no one there.

"Looks like we'll have to stay here all night, Emma," Billy laughed.

"That's fine with me, Mr. Tankersly," Emma said in the sexiest voice Billy had ever heard. He wanted to just curl up and spend the night with Emma right here in the boat. They had the keys to the motor, and after looking around for a place to leave them, Billy came back to the boat telling Emma, no luck.

The two laughed about it, holding each other tightly as the waves kept rocking the boat, and they had not sat down yet. Finally, they sat on the same bench in the boat. Billy looked at Emma and could not resist drawing her close and kissing her. The kiss was the most exciting thing ever in Billy's life. He opened his eyes while they were still kissing and saw a zillion stars in the sky as there were no lights around. Billy knew life could never get better! All of a sudden, a flashlight shined on them, and a voice in the dark said, "I forgot about this boat being out, once it got dark," the man who rented them the boat blared out.

After the shock wore off, Billy handed the man the keys, telling him they had decided to stay all night to protect his property as there was no place to leave the keys.

"Yeah, you kids would have enjoyed that, but what about your parents?" the man said, laughing.

"They probably would have been worried sick," Billy said in a serious voice. "We are so glad you remembered and came back."

Billy and Emma walked to the car with Emma laughing hysterically. "You are so funny, Billy."

On the way back to his hotel, Billy drove Emma's car as slow as possible, just to spend more time with her. When they reached the hotel, they sat in the parking lot for close to an hour, telling each other how much they would miss the other.

There was no doubt, Billy had fallen in love with Emma and Emma with him. She agreed to come to as many games as she could, and Billy offered to pay for each of the flights. He knew he would have to clear it with John Hopkins, his financial adviser. They had agreed on Billy having a specific portion of his bonus money tied up in investments. But, Billy was so infatuated with Emma that he'd push to get any money necessary to see Emma during the season. Billy already told her that next winter, he would be living in Lexington to be with her.

As usual, Billy was flying to Spring Training early to get a jump on the other position players. He knew he would have to leave Emma and start focusing on baseball.

His last day with her, he confessed that he might not be the best boyfriend long term because he was so focused on breaking Ricky Henderson's stolen base record.

"1406," she replied.

"You know that Emma?" he asked startled.

"Of course, silly," she replied. "You don't think you are the only one who studies stats?" she asked, with again, a sexy flirting voice.

"Emma quit it. You are making me to completely forget baseball. Seriously, how did you really know Ricky's stolen base record?" he asked.

Emma laughed again, tossing her long blonde hair off her shoulder.

"You really want the truth?" she smiled.

Before he could answer, she told him that Bobby, when he stayed with the Williams last year, had done nothing but talk about his best friend, Billy Tankersly.

"Really, Emma, Bobby told you?" he asked.

"Not only did Bobby tell me, he told me if I ever bet on anything, make a bet on you because there was no doubt in his mind, you were going to break Ricky's mark," she continued.

"You have no idea how much Bobby loves you, Billy," Emma added.

"Yeah, we've been best friends since 1st grade. When he moved to Austin, I cried, and then did everything, every year to find a way to get to Austin. It turned out that my travel team manager had figured a way for us to play in a tournament in Austin. Until now, that had to be one of my best feelings ever, arriving in Austin and seeing Bobby beneath the big Hyatt Regency sign," Billy excitedly told Emma about his trip.

"But, seeing you in the moonlight on the lake, and kissing you, Emma, will be my new most exciting thing ever," Billy confessed. "I'm going to really miss you, as he pulled her close again for what might be their final kiss before his mind had to return to his goal.

He was getting ready to get his Uber app out when Emma called.

"Hey Billy," she gushed. "Dad let me off to take you to the airport." She picked him up ten minutes later, driving as slow as possible, but talking baseball to him all the way to the airport. She was encouraging him to "get out there and beat Skip out." They kissed one last time before Billy had to check in. Her last words were, "You will be on the Royals this year, Billy." What a perfect send-off. He appreciated Emma's attitude and words more than he could even imagine. Before he realized it, he was in the air on his way to Spring Training.

31

Will Billy Beat Out Skip

"What an amazing feeling," Billy thought as he put his metal spikes on in the clubhouse.

"Hey Billy," came a voice from across the clubhouse. Billy recognized it immediately.

"Bobby, he shouted," seeing his best friend. "You came early too?" Billy asked, or commented, he wasn't sure which.

"This is great, Billy," said Bobby as he hugged his best friend. "I may not make it to the Royals this year, but soon, I'll be joining you."

"I'm not even sure I'll make the Royals this year, Bobby. "Skip Anderson is back healthy and has one more year on his contract."

"I will have to beat Skip out, which will be hard because of the size of his contract. The Royals will have to start Skip, and that leaves no room for me," Billy said in a voice that Bobby knew was Billy sharing his innermost feelings.

"Well, if anyone can, it's you, Billy," Bobby said in a tone Billy remembered hearing over Skype many times as Bobby would always encourage Billy, even if it was about mowing lawns.

The two ran on the field to be greeted by hugs from all of the Royals pitchers and catchers.

Bobby could see that the Royals players in camp also thought Billy could beat Skip out, just in the way they treated Billy. They all seemed to admire Bobby's 18-year-old best friend.

The two position players played catch in the outfield until Ace Gurruara yelled to Billy.

"Give us someone to throw to, you two guys out there doing nothing," Ace kidded them.

Billy knew Bobby had not faced a major league pitcher, so he told his best friend to go first.

"Who is this?" Ace asked as Bobby stepped into the box. "Your worst enemy," Bobby replied in a cocky way for a guy facing his first big leaguer.

Ace laughed and immediately threw a 95 mph fastball at Bobby.

Bobby swung, and Ace turned to see how far over the centerfield fence the ball traveled.

He turned to Bobby saying, "Are you a new guy on the Royals, I hope."

Bobby sheepishly said, "No, Mr. Gurruara, I'm just trying to make the team."

After several more pitches and Bobby hitting two more out of the park, it was Billy's turn to face Ace.

"Finally, I've got someone I can pitch to, who won't be bombing hits over the fence," Ace laughed. Then he added, "Good job new guy."

Bobby was thrilled. He'd hit three over the fence against a major league pitcher. "What could be better?" Bobby thought to himself, as he watched Billy in the cage.

Billy sent line drive after line drive to all parts of the field.

"OK Ace, we know it's your first day, so we'll take it easy on you the next time in the cage," Billy yelled at the man who had played at least five years in the majors.

Billy and Bobby walked back to the dugout, and Billy introduced him to Guma Gomez, the lefty reliever who was working on his glove. Then Johy Tripoz jumped over the step in the dugout and almost fell. Guma started laughing, but Billy introduced

Bobby to Johy. Before the day was over, Bobby had met all the pitchers and catchers in camp.

Billy and Bobby continued to be the only batters facing the pitchers because the position players had not arrived in camp yet. Finally, several others started walking in. The first player Billy saw was his friend from the Storm Chasers, Mack.

"Bobby, I want you to meet Mack, the fearless second baseman of the Omaha Storm Chasers," Billy said with a half-smile. He knew Mack was in no mood to hear about Omaha. He was here to make the Royals this year.

More and more of the position players arrived. Billy introduced Bobby to each. Bobby was in 7th heaven, but he had a job to do, and that was to make the Royals like his best friend had last year.

The camp was no different than last year. The first two weeks, it seemed like there were a hundred ballplayers on the field, all trying to make, or stay with the Royals, but Billy knew that would change in a couple of days when the majority of the players in camp would be assigned to Omaha or Lexington.

"Someone like Ted Barns, who had played on the Royals for three years, but was approaching 36 years old, might not even make the club this year," Billy thought. It was a scary time for many, hoping to stay in the major league camp, but knowing that only the very best would spend the rest of Spring Training playing on the Royals. Billy wondered about himself and Bobby.

On the 10th day in camp, many were sent to the minor league areas to practice. But Billy, Mack, and Bobby were still on the Royals roster.

Billy did not have a good Spring Training, in the field or at bat. For the first time in his life, he had things on his mind, other than baseball. Emma Williams to be precise. He could not shake the image of them kissing on the boat. The only part of his game that flourished was his base running. He was put in as a pinch runner a couple of times and stole second base easily both times.

It was down to the final days before the Royals broke camp. Billy was on the 40 man roster, but that did not mean he would make the 25 man active roster. Because this was really his rookie season since he'd only played a few games last year, there was a good chance he would be sent to Omaha.

"Billy, what do you think?" Bobby asked. "Will I make it this year?"

"I honestly think your chances are better than mine right now," Billy confessed. "My gosh, the way you've been hitting HR's almost every day since camp started, and even in the games, you've been playing great," Billy told Bobby.

"They put me on the 40 man roster, what does that mean, Billy?" Bobby asked.

"That is great, Bobby. That means both of us are on the 40 man roster even if we don't make the 25 man active roster. We could be playing at Omaha together, but get called up during the year," Billy smiled, not really wanting to go back to the minor leagues. He knew he needed a great Spring Training to beat out Skip for the starting position at SS.

Two days later, camp broke, and Billy, Bobby, and Mack would soon find out their fate. Billy felt one of the three would be on the active roster.

"Who?" he thought.

"Would he be able to add stolen bases to his quest to beat Ricky, or be back at Omaha?" he thought to himself.

32

The Last Day of Camp

Today was the day, he would find out his fate. He was scared. He wanted so badly to stay up in the bigs, after his experience last year. He felt his chances were good. He decided to call Emma, to get his mind off the decision he would learn about in two hours.

"Hey, Billy, what's up?" she asked, knowing he had not called her at all during spring training.

"They are announcing today who will stay with the Royals and who won't," Billy sighed, pretty sure he already knew the answer after his less than stellar spring training.

"Honey, keep your confidence level up," she said.

Billy was stunned. She called him "honey." He couldn't believe what was going on in his mind. He was thinking, "Maybe being sent back to Lexington would be the best thing for me." Billy was shocked at his own thinking. For his first 18 years, all he'd thought about was baseball, and now he was thinking more about Emma.

"Emma, I've really missed you," he confessed. "I can't get the thought of us kissing in the boat out of my mind," he added, feeling like that was the biggest confession he'd ever made. He was shocked that he'd actually admitted it to Emma.

"Billy, I've missed you too, but let's get one thing straight, I want to help you reach Ricky's record, not distract from it," Emma told him, in an almost scolding manner for his comment about how much he'd thought of and missed her.

He wasn't sure if what she'd just said was positive or negative. Did that mean she wasn't happy that he'd been thinking of her?

"Emma, how are you going to help me break Ricky's mark if I can't even play in the majors?" he asked, trying to figure out what exactly she meant.

"Billy, listen closely to me. Whether you make the Royals out of Spring Training is not the most important thing. What is most important is that you keep your mind on what you have to do to reach the majors full time, where you can be starting. You and I both know, Skip has another year on his contract, and it would be hard for the Royals not to start him every game. That means you might get sent back to Omaha, or end up sitting on the bench for the Royals. Maybe you and Bobby will get to play with each other again," she added.

For the first time in a week, Billy felt peaceful. Emma was right. No matter what happened today, he still intended to break Ricky's stolen base record.

The End

Be sure to read the next book in the Metal Spikes series.

Billy And Bobby
in
METAL SPIKES III

The first two chapters begin on the next page.

1

A Surprise in Des Moines

Billy suited up in his Storm Chaser uniform. Coach Keller explained why Billy had been sent down. Like Billy suspected, it was because the Royals had to stick with their high-paying shortstop, Skip Anderson. He explained to Billy that he would more than likely be the first player called up if there was an injury, but the Royals did not want Billy to be sitting on the bench every day.

"Hey Billy," Bobby shouted from across the diamond. Throw me a low one so I can practice scooping it up."

Bobby was now playing 1B for the Storm Chasers and was told by the Royals that there was a chance he could be called up this year. The Royals had been spending money on an Urban Baseball Camp for African American's because of the fall-off in black boys coming to baseball. It seemed most African Americans were playing more basketball and football rather than baseball. With Bobby being the only African American close to being ready for the big time in the Royals minor leagues, they were anxious to see Bobby have a good year where they could promote him as soon as he was ready.

Both young men were looked upon by the Royals as part of the future of the franchise. Mack had been sent down too, and Billy knew the Royals were looking at him as their future at 2B.

"Maybe all three of them would be playing on the Royals by the end of the year," Billy thought, as he tossed one low throw after another toward Bobby at

1B in their first practice session since arriving in Omaha.

The Storm Chasers would be playing their first game against the Iowa Cubs, the Triple A club of the Chicago Cubs. Their opening series was to be played at Principal Stadium in Des Moines.

As the two young men rode the team bus from Omaha to Des Moines, which was only two hours from Omaha, they talked about Spring Training, about the coming year, and of course, Emma.

"Bobby, I've never really thanked you for not asking Emma out," Billy started, realizing he and Bobby had not talked about Emma since arriving in Surprise, Arizona for Spring Training or here in Omaha.

"What was the point?" Bobby stated. All she did when we were together was talk about you."

"Really, Bobby," Billy laughed. "She told me that when the two of you were together, all you did was talk about me."

"You are the one who told me not to ask her out," Bobby said with a frown on his face.

Billy laughed at his best friend.

"Would you have asked her out if I'd not said anything?" Billy asked.

"Is Austin the Capital of Texas?" Bobby laughed. "Heck yes, I would have. She is the most beautiful girl I've ever met, and she is a baseball fan."

"Yep, she is both," Billy said, thinking about Emma now and not their upcoming season opener.

"I haven't had time to tell you, Bobby, but I flew to Lexington before going to Spring Training, and we had our first date," Billy was now excited to be talking about Emma again. He'd called her after getting the news that he was being sent down to Omaha. She told him to keep his mind on baseball because she wanted to watch him steal his 1,407th base some year in the future.

"Bobby, I think I'm in love with Emma," Billy finally told his best friend.

"Really, Billy?" Bobby asked, in a serious mood because he had not heard about Billy dating Emma until now, at least not from Billy.

"We spent a lot of time talking, about baseball, you, fishing," Billy started.

"Fishing?" Bobby interrupted.

Billy told Bobby about renting the boat, fishing all day, and getting back to the dock so late that the owner of the boat had already left. He shared with his best friend about sitting in the boat with Emma, thinking they might be there all night.

"That was the first time I'd kissed her, Bobby," Billy started, thinking more about Emma than his upcoming game.

"Billy, do not let a girl get in the way of you breaking Ricky's record," Bobby warned.

"Yeah, I hear you, buddy," Billy said, still thinking about Emma.

The bus arrived in Des Moines in time for dinner. As they exited the bus, Billy saw her, standing off on the curb. He had to do a double take to make sure that was really Emma.

"Bobby, Emma is here," he shouted to his best bud.

Bobby laughed.

Billy went running over to Emma, lifting her up and swinging her around. He really didn't care what the other players thought.

"What are you doing here?" Billy asked in disbelief that she was really here.

"Well, your best friend called me and asked if I could drive up from Lexington to see you guys in your first game," she answered.

"Bobby did that?" he asked, stunned.

Bobby was now by their side, giving Emma a hug, thanking her for coming.

Billy was confused. What was his best friend giving Emma a hug when he'd just told him that he thought he was in love with this girl?

"Emma, you will be happy to know that all during Spring Training, Billy did not mention your name once," Bobby started.

Billy wondered, "What exactly is going on here?"

She hugged Billy again and kissed him in front of Bobby and the few team members who had not gone into the hotel yet.

"Billy, I couldn't help myself. I texted Bobby during Spring Training to ask how you were doing," Emma started explaining. We texted back and forth several times, and I had to tell Bobby about our first kiss."

"What?" Billy looked at Bobby as he was talking. "You mean you let me talk about Emma, telling you about our first kiss when you already knew.

Bobby laughed louder than Billy had ever heard him laugh.

"You have no idea how hard it was to keep a straight face as you were telling me," Bobby cackled.

The three walked arm in arm into the restaurant, where the rest of the team was. As they entered, everyone stood and started clapping. Billy was stunned. Did the entire team know?

"Yes, I told everyone about Emma showing up tonight, and how surprised you'd be, and asked them all to not mention it to you," Bobby told his best friend.

After dinner, the three of them talked a while, before Bobby said, "hey kids, it's time Billy and I get to bed. We've got a game tomorrow," Bobby said in a joking way, but also serious.

Billy walked Emma to her room and then settled down in his room, thinking about Emma and then reminding himself that breaking Ricky's record was more important than anything else.

He dozed off to sleep thinking about getting three hits in the season opener tomorrow and making the Royals call him up sooner than they had imagined, and maybe marrying Emma along the way.

2

First Game Of The Season

Billy's first thought as he saw the lineup card with him batting third and Bobby cleanup, was how similar it seemed to their first game together on the Rockets when they were both nine years old.

Mack was leading off with Arturo Cruz, playing left field, hitting second. Billy had his bat in his hand as the first pitch was thrown to Mack.

"Ball one," bellowed the umpire, who Billy remembered from last year.

One the next pitch, Mack hit a ground ball between SS and 3B, and no one was able to reach it.

"Way to start the season, Mack," yelled Billy getting ready to step into the on deck circle, still wishing he was in the leadoff spot and wanting to steal. He looked up into the crowd to see if he could find Emma. Before he could spot her, Arturo hit a line drive to left field that was walloped, and Mack had to stop at 2B. Billy forgot about Emma. His only thought, "Get a hit to drive in the first run of the season."

He watched the first pitch, a fastball, hit the outside corner of the plate. He didn't even need to hear the umpire signaling the pitch was a strike.

He turned around, remembering Art Brown, the umpire, who was the first person in a game to congratulate him last year after being promoted to the Storm Chasers. "Hey ump, you know that was a ball," he laughed, stepping out of the box.

"Don't give me any trouble, hotshot," Art Brown returned the banter.

With two strikes on him, Billy choked up about ½ inch on the bat. He was expecting a curve, and as he watched the spin from the pitcher's hand, he knew he'd guessed right. He swung hard and ended up hitting a slug bunt that bounced high in the air, giving him enough time to beat the throw to first base.

Now the bases were loaded for Bobby. Billy had not seen Bobby play in a game since the travel squad went to Austin for a tournament, but he'd seen enough of his power in Spring Training to know the pitcher better not give Bobby the same pitch he threw to him. He did, and Bobby hit the first pitch over the left field wall by 30 feet. Bobby had just hit his first Grand Slam HR in a Storm Chaser uniform.

As Bobby rounded the bases, Mack, Arturo, and Billy all waited at the plate to congratulate Bobby. The Storm Chasers led 4-0, and the Cubs pitcher had not gotten a single out. The Cubs pitching coach walked to the mound to try to steady Goose Tyson, the starting pitcher. Tyson was up in the big leagues about the same amount of time as Billy last year, so Billy knew this was not the usual Goose Tyson.

After the pitching coach's visit to the mound, Goose settled down and struck out the next three Omaha hitters.

Billy and the rest of the Storm Chasers took the field in the bottom of the first. It was fun playing with Bobby again, especially after seeing his best friend hit one so far out of the park that Tyson didn't even turn around to watch it. He knew from the sound of the bat hitting the ball that he'd never see that ball again. He forgot that the Storm Chasers bullpen was behind the fence, and after the game, won by the Storm Chases, 5-1, the relievers who had been in the bullpen gave Bobby his first professional Grand Slam baseball. They seemed to be more excited about giving Bobby the ball than he was in hitting it.

"It is going to be a fun year, Billy thought," hoping he, Mack and Bobby would be called up to the Royals by the time the All-Star break occurred, but for now, Billy was a Storm Chaser and he knew what he had to do to get called up. Steal bases.

About the Author

Warren Haskin grew up on the outskirts of Kansas City in Mission, Kansas. When he became a Cub Scout, his Dad and several other fathers obtained land at the edge of town to build a baseball diamond for their sons. It was truly the first Field of Dreams. From that moment on, Warren's dream was to be good enough to play major league ball.

He played college baseball in the Big 12 for the University of Kansas Jayhawks and for the Navy in a semi-pro league in Memphis, Tennessee, but his dream changed directions when he married. As a young husband and father of two, he embarked on a life-long career as an entrepreneur developing personal growth programs using much of what he'd learned from baseball.

Warren's passion for the sport has remained throughout his life. He has been a player, coach, sports editor, baseball and football announcer, business developer and owner, and trainer.

This is Warren's second fiction book. Like in Metal Spikes I, his inspirational teaching shows from the first to the last chapter through the "coaches," along the way, who teach young people and adults how to succeed.

He currently resides in Austin, Texas and is a business and personal consultant for Help People, Inc. He can be reached at whaskin@HelpPeople.com.

Made in the USA
Middletown, DE
07 December 2020

25400242R00116